NO FOOTPRINTS

NO FOOTPRINTS

A DARCY LOTT MYSTERY

SUSAN DUNLAP

COUNTERPOINT
BERKELEY

Library of Congress Cataloging-in-Publication Data is available

ISBN: 978-1-58243-771-2

Cover Design by Domini Dragoone
Interior Design by www.meganjonesdesign.com

COUNTERPOINT
1919 Fifth Street
Berkeley, CA 94710
www.counterpointpress.com

Distributed by Publishers Group West

10 9 8 7 6 5 4 3 2 1

For Susan Sandler

WHEN LIFE IS too good, I get wary.

I *was* wary—guardedly thrilled that not only was I the go-to stunt double on *Faster!* but I was the one doing the final location scan on this site I'd pushed for—the Golden Gate Bridge with the evening fog flowing in. Now the mother of all fogs loomed just to the west. It was perfect for me running the walkway, noting the effect on light, visibility, mobility, so we could update the storyboards for the scenes here. With luck—

But I already had so much good luck I must've been siphoning it from strangers.

Best of all, Mike, my brother who'd been missing for twenty years, was finally home. Right now he was driving across the bridge in a snazzy silver convertible with the top down! When I made it to the Marin side, he'd be waiting. And in four short days the whole family'd be at Mom's for the celebration we'd feared would never come, Mike's birthday dinner with him cutting his cake. I was so happy it positively terrified me.

I'd passed the first bridge tower minutes ago, moving through the November cold as fast as I could while still being able to check out the walkway surface, the railings to the roadway, and the water. I'd guessed the towers would provide some shelter and they did. Fingers of fog were wagging across the roadway and parts of the city were already covered, but

I could still see San Francisco glowing in the last dazzle before dusk. Even here on the walkway there were good visibility breaks in the fog. Two guys in parkas leaned against the railing in one of the alcoves, arms around each other's shoulders. In the next alcove a tourist took a last picture, packed up his camera, and headed fast for land as if he'd just realized how frigid it was going to be once the sun was really gone. It'd be a long mile back to the city side.

That view had been my selling point. There'd be raised cameras on the far walk, shooting over the traffic and across the running double—me—catching the sharp glow of the city in last light in the distance.

Something grazed my arm. *Pay attention, Darcy!* I skirted a propped bike, barely missing two women trying to zip their jackets without slowing down.

On the roadway, cars clopped over the gratings, icy wind rushing between them. I should have worn a cap. I hadn't. Now my long hair lashed my face.

I glanced up. The dense fog wall was at the far side of the bridge.

Mike ought to have passed by now. Where was he? I checked the roadway but it was useless. Couldn't he have found a brighter car? Yellow like the warning jacket the bike patrol wears, or red, like the bridge itself, or even darker red, like the coat on a woman ahead of me on the walkway. Maybe he'd already gone by. I'd started out running too fast; now I was paying the price, but I'd never let him, of all people, see me slowing down after a mere mile.

Was that a horn?

It was! I turned in time to see Mike wave.

The woman in the red coat—red *jacket*—jerked toward him with a big, surprised smile. Did she know him? Headlights bounced off her, revealing a snazzy drum major's jacket complete with buttons and braid. A notice-me jacket. With the wind snapping her black hair, she looked terrific. Even I could barely take my eyes off her.

But she didn't wave back or give a nod of recognition. She looked, even from a distance, shocked.

Then the headlights were gone and she disappeared into the dark. I turned to look for Mike. He'd accelerated forward into the fog.

Headlights hit the woman again. She was leaning against the red metal railing looking at the view, her body in her red jacket blending into it. The bridge was almost entirely in fog now, but the city was spotlighted gold. As if it were rising up to meet the last ray of sun. As if—

Omigod!

"No!"

She wasn't sightseeing! She was putting down her purse and reaching for the railing. She was going to climb over. She was going to jump!

"No! Wait! WAIT!" She was a few car lengths ahead. I ran full out, but I wasn't picking up speed.

She snapped toward me. Headlights flashed on her face. Her mouth was quivering so violently I could see it at this distance. She looked heart-breakingly sad and, at the same time, panicked. For a moment our gazes met. She started toward me.

Then, as if catching herself, she jerked her head toward the water, bent down, picked up her purse, and tossed it over the railing.

No! "No! Wait! Don't!" I was screaming, but there was no way she could hear me, not over the wind and the cars. She was ten yards away.

She hoisted herself up on the railing.

Why didn't they make it higher? Four feet, that's nothing! I pushed my legs faster. It was like I wasn't moving at all. Like I was running in slow motion. Like everything around me was slo-mo. The wind was slapping my hair, holding it out before it hit my face. The fog fuzzed the edges of everything. The woman was shifting oh so slowly, slightly back and forth on the cold railing two hundred forty feet above the water.

Her leg slipped over it and down the far side.

"Stop!"

She was sitting on top, as if astride a horse.

"*Stop!*"

She leaned forward almost parallel to the walkway, pulling her other leg up. She was on the railing, *lying* on it.

The wind itself could blow her over. The suicide call box was right here, and the cameras. Why didn't the Bridge cops see her?

I was gasping. My legs felt like lead. *Hurry, dammit!*

She was slipping off.

"Hang on!" I shouted. "Don't move! You're okay!" Only another few steps and I could grab her. "I'm coming!"

She slid over the side. I caught my breath. The metal catwalk there was a couple of feet wide. A place for suicides to stand and think. The last step into eternity, somebody'd called it.

She was poised there, turned away from the bridge, toward the water. She was still holding on. Ahead of her was nothing but air, and water.

I lunged for her.

She jerked forward, out of reach.

I caught her jacket.

The snaps unsnapped; the jacket went loose.

She struggled to get free. All that was holding her was cloth.

Frantically, I pulled back on the jacket, the button biting into my hand.

The fabric slipped, and she was wriggling her arms out. In a moment she'd pull loose, the jacket would slip right off, and she'd fall.

No matter how tightly I held it, she'd fall.

I had to grab her body. I had to *let go* and grab.

If I misjudged—

I yanked hard on the fabric. She jerked back into me. I let go, flung my arms forward, and slammed them around her chest. I grabbed my own wrist and held on.

I was half over the rail, my knees jammed against the uprights, panting, gasping.

She braced her legs, thrust her shoulders forward.

My hands were slipping. With every bit of strength I had left, I braced my own knees and rammed my hands into her ribs.

She let out a scream, then slammed back against me, elbows flying. Her head smacked hard into mine.

My arms went numb. I couldn't feel my hands. From memory alone my one hand was connected to the other wrist. But in a minute that would fail.

"Let me go! I have to—"

Praying my grip would still hold, I leaned back and pulled with everything I had.

She came flying back over the rail and we toppled together onto the cement walk. My head hit it so hard I couldn't see. I could feel her pushing free. I tried to hang on, but my hands weren't working at all now. I could barely breathe.

She managed to stand. Her pale, terrified face loomed above me. She looked as stunned as I was. It was like a moment beyond time. Her black hair was snapping in the wind. Across her eyes emotions flashed and were gone, one after another, instant after instant.

She reached toward me, as if to thank me. But something stopped her and she turned away. When she turned back her expression had changed.

She leaned in close and said, "I did one decent thing in my life and you ruined it. Now it's going to be harder, but I have to . . . By the weekend I'll be dead."

2

IN AN INSTANT, she was gone.

My head swirled, my hands and feet were pins and needles. I tried to push myself up but couldn't. Desperately I strained to make out footsteps—her walking away, running even, but the cars clanked too loud over the roadway grates. I was struggling to hear—to *not* hear—a splash. As if! Two hundred and forty feet down!

In a minute I was over and on my knees, and staring at something red. Her jacket! The red jacket with the brass buttons was lying there abandoned.

What did that mean? Had she run a few yards one way or the other, climbed over the railing there, and jumped? I shot glances in both directions. No sight of her.

She could have climbed over and still been on the apron, clinging to the slippery rail. It was a foot lower than the walkway. Maybe she was on the far side . . . But if she changed her mind, climbing *back* over the railing wasn't easy. It'd be a *five-*foot barrier then. *Oh, God!* I peered into the fog. I couldn't make out a form. I eased back off my knees, braced my legs, stood, staggered over to the railing, and stared down.

By the weekend I'll be dead. Unless she had a change of heart, she'd be back to try again tomorrow. Or the next day, or the next. Without me here to save her. I squinted into the thick gray, looking both ways, willing my eyes to spot her. Visibility was terrible. Looking down, as if . . .

Hands pressed in on my shoulders, not hard, but definitely firm. "Let's move back from the railing!" a man urged, in an official tone.

"What?" How long had he been behind me? I hadn't even heard him come up. His arm slipped around my shoulder with firm authority. I could feel myself being hauled back like a boat into dry dock.

"I'm okay," I insisted, looking over at the Bridge Patrol guy. He was staring at me. Hard. "*I'm* not the jumper. You saw it all on camera? The woman in red? Saw her almost jump?"

He gave an "I'm listening, not committing" nod.

"You had to have seen it. Why else would you be here? You weren't just out for a ride."

"We saw the fight."

"Fight! I pulled her back. If I hadn't, she'd be in the water!"

"We appreciate that." But his tone didn't reassure me.

My head still throbbed, but suddenly the urgency struck me. "'*I did one decent thing in my life and you ruined it!*' That's what she said. '*You ruined it!*' She hasn't given up! I don't have time to convince you," I stormed at him. "I need to find her. She could be hoisting herself over the railing again right now!" I checked both directions—not a soul. Great clumps of fog shoved across the roadway. Cars in the far lanes were invisible.

"Look, it's a fluke I even saw her! Just luck I was running along here now. No sane person's on the bridge this late. She could be a hundred yards away climbing over the railing right now. Or there's tomorrow night. We have to find her!"

"We're alert."

Whatever that meant! He was still eyeing me. Now I took him in. He wasn't what I'd have expected. McNin—the name on his laminated

ID—wasn't much taller than me, wiry, with brown hair, angular face, and eyes that indicated they'd seen a lot.

"Believe me," I repeated. "I'm not the one who came here to jump."

He sighed just loudly enough so I caught it.

"Hey, I've got a brother waiting for me on the Marin side. He's probably already left me three messages by now. Do I need to prove it to you?"

"I'm just concerned for you."

"Be concerned about *her*. You saw us hit the ground, right? Saw her get up and . . . Where'd she go? She didn't—"

"Go over? No. Not here, anyway. Not near our cameras. I didn't pass her, so she must've headed back toward the city."

"Then we've still got time!"

"Yeah." He sighed again. "So, who're we looking for?"

"I don't know her name."

"Describe her."

"Red jacket—"

"Like the one you're holding?"

"It's hers. She left it behind. I'd been grabbing hold of it."

"So, we're hunting a woman *not* wearing a red jacket. *Not* wearing the most visible thing."

"I guess." My head still throbbed.

"Go on."

"Let me think. Dark hair, chin-length. I was so caught by the jacket . . . but underneath . . . Okay, yeah. White T-shirt, fitted, and black pants—slacks, not jeans—"

"How—"

"I didn't notice the pants per se, like I would have if they hadn't gone with the jacket. Jeans would have been a whole different look."

9

He eyed the tights and long-sleeved T-shirt I'd grabbed for the run and was now shivering in, but said nothing.

"Listen, we can catch her. How many people are out here this late in a T-shirt? Wait, I remembered something. She had a purse but she dropped it . . . over."

"How?"

"She leaned over and tossed it."

"Did she watch it fall?"

"Nuh uh. She let it go and then took hold of the rail to climb over. Why?"

Suddenly he was all action. "Get in." He motioned to the open-air cart.

"The purse? Why does the purse matter?"

"Come on! Get in! Look, the last thing jumpers want is to see how long it takes to hit the water. How long *does* it? *Forever!* That's what survivors say. Plenty of time to wonder if everything they've heard about hitting the water at seventy miles per hour's true. Jumpers are looking for oblivion and those four seconds before they hit, they're the dead opposite—an eternity of regret, fear, and helplessness. You strapped in?"

"How fast does this thing go?" We were more than a mile from the city side. We had time. But not spare time.

He stepped on the accelerator and we sped off, fast enough through the fog to make my teeth chatter. The hum of the engine seemed to fight the *rat-a-tat* of the passing cars and trucks, and the wind from them was like a finger snapping repeatedly against my right ear. McNin was saying something but I couldn't hear. Already my face was icy. We whipped along the empty walkway. Ahead I could barely make out the giant red ladder of the south tower.

"That her?" He spat out the words and hit the brake. If I hadn't been buckled in, I'd've sailed off.

"Where? Oh, there. Can't tell. Move closer."

"Don't want to spook her. Is it her?"

I wanted it to be her; I willed it to be. I leaned closer, as if a couple inches would help. "I don't think so. That's not a T-shirt, it's a hoodie. And I think . . . yeah, those are jeans she's wearing."

"Damn."

From the roadway, headlights hit my eyes and vanished: bright—black, bright—black. I could barely make out shapes in the murk.

"Her?" He was slowing again, indicating a long-haired woman with a tall man.

"She wouldn't have brought a friend!"

"Just look!"

"Too small. She was my height—five seven—you must've seen that."

"S'okay, we've still got a chance." He was like a rescue dog, wholly into it now.

He whipped around two male joggers. We'd almost reached the south tower. The great red metal supports leapt out at us. McNin cut sharply left as the walkway angled around the tower.

"She won't be here," I said. "If she jumped here, she'd hit the cement apron."

"People do."

People do! People jump and hit the cement base at God-knows-how-many miles per hour! No wonder McNin was hot to find her.

"But she won't be jumping beyond this."

"How come? Oh." I spotted the hurricane fencing above the railing. "Ah, that's to keep jumpers from—"

"To keep them from landing on the workers below!"

"Jesus!"

"Believe it."

"Keep going! We can still catch her."

"Hang on." He stamped on the accelerator. We whipped along the empty walkway to its end and stopped. "That's it," he said. "She could have parked any of six places, gone down to Fort Point, under the roadway to the lot, or anywhere along Lincoln Boulevard. Or she could be walking through the Presidio."

The Presidio! Nearly 1,500 acres, a lot of it wooded. There'd never been a San Franciscan who wasn't pleased this spectacular former army base had survived since 1776 intact. Until us, now. "If she made it in among those eucalypts, she's gone."

"Yeah. It's good, though," he said, as if convincing himself. "Good she's already made her try . . . November . . ."

"Busy?"

"Start of the holidays, the lonely season. If you've got family you're out of touch with, parties you're not invited to, no plans—"

"'By the weekend I'll be dead.' That's what she said." Suddenly I was so cold I felt like my skin would shatter. But I couldn't give up, not now, not yet. "What about the bathroom?"

"Over there."

I checked. Empty. Reality was setting in. "I just can't believe," I said, stepping back onto the cart, "that I could pull her back from the edge and then have her just disappear. Like she never existed."

"That's the lure of the bridge. No mess, no pain, no consequences. Or so they think."

"Yeah, sure, no pain, maybe for them. For the family—waiting, never knowing—pain doesn't let up." I was thinking, of course, of Mike's disappearance and Mom never leaving the house for more than a day in those two decades lest he should come home and find no one there. Thinking of the false hopes, the deadening disappointments, the numbness. Of never crossing the Golden Gate Bridge without wondering . . . of my favorite brother who'd vanished and stayed gone twenty years, and of the stranger wearing his skin whom we'd finally found. But this woman . . . "I just can't believe we could lose her. There's got to be something—Wait. A bicycle. Maybe in the fog—did you see it?"

"No. Definitely no. That's something we note."

"I passed one, about a hundred yards before I spotted her. No rider near it."

"If it's gone—good sign. Not a bad sign anyway."

"What about those joggers we just passed? They must've seen her."

"Okay, but . . ." He shrugged. But he started back to the cart with what seemed like hope.

We caught them a hundred yards onto the bridge. I soon realized why McNin had shrugged. "A woman? On a bike?" The taller guy mused. "Maybe. Dunno. Didn't get in our way."

The short one was running in place. "We're focused. We got held up this afternoon; now we're really late. We were pressing. When we do this bit, we don't even see the skyline. Like I say, we're focused."

McNin took their contact info, but the look he gave me said "dead end."

"So," he said after a moment, "you want a ride back to this most patient brother of yours on the other side?"

Omigod! All those years Mike was gone, never a day had gone by without my thinking of him, and now here he was waiting for me and I'd totally forgotten. "Thanks." As we drove north I turned on the phone and mea culpa'd to his voicemail, "But a nice cop's speeding me toward you so turn on the heater for me."

It was quarter to six. Dusk had passed to night, and, as often happens, the wind had suddenly eased up. In fifteen minutes the walkway'd be closed. The ride was easier now—clear of pedestrians. Even so, it was still Arctic, with both of us shivering. For the first time I looked beyond the railing to catch a glimpse of the city skyline. Nothing but gray now. When he slowed to skirt the north tower, I said, "How can people jump in this kind of weather? It's so—"

"They go all the time. *All* the time. Two, three a month, and those are the ones we know of. The water"—he was shouting over the noise—"it's deceiving. Looks warm and soft, brown. Like they'll land easy, like floating down to a nice pillow. But if you'd seen those bodies . . ."

I couldn't bear to think about that. "McNin, she said I'd ruined it. She said she'd be dead by the weekend. D'you believe her?"

He slowed the cart. "She could go either way. Take this as a wake-up call. Or just get more pissed and be back like she promised. No way to tell. Not with what little we know of her."

"I just can't believe—"

He put a hand on my shoulder. "Believe."

I clutched her red jacket tighter to me, uselessly. It was ridiculous to be freezing and not put it on, but how could I?

Almost in slow motion it seemed now we rolled onto the Marin side. The parking lot was nearly empty. There was a young couple curled around each other on a bench, and one bent-over old guy in a watch cap at the bus stop. None of them were even facing the water. "There," I said, "that silver convertible." The top was now up.

"You want me to explain to your brother?"

"Nah. I'm a big girl. But listen, thanks. Will you keep an eye out?"

"I'll let you know."

I extricated a card.

"Stunts. Hey, I'm impressed."

"Call me. I'll get you a set pass. You'll be bored 99 percent of the time, but the other one could be dynamite."

He looked down at the card again, then up, and finally said, "Okay then, huh?" If only the woman we'd been searching for knew how much we cared. Slowly, he guided the cart toward Mike's car.

I expected to find Mike slumped behind the wheel, expected to hear Black Rebel Motorcycle Club running down the battery, expected the heater to be on blast. But the car was silent and empty. "He's probably in the john. I've kept him waiting long enough."

"I can stay with—"

"I'm fine. But you'll let me know if you hear anything. Anything! If you even have any idea, right?"

"Yeah." With that, he pulled loose, turned the cart around, and sped off, leaving me alone with the cold and all my fears. I could still feel her body against my chest as I heaved her back. She couldn't just disappear and . . . die! Suddenly, I was desperate to get out of here, back to the warmth of Mom's kitchen.

To life.

I tried the car door—locked, dammit! What was this about? We never used to lock cars. I moved to the downwind side, squatted for what little protection the vehicle could offer, and pulled out my phone to see how many messages he'd left. I was just putting finger to key when the old man I'd noticed began hunching toward me. Did he want to know why Bridge Patrol dropped me here? Or was the guy just hoping for a ride? Did he—

It wasn't till he was nearly to the car that I recognized him.

3

"OMIGOD!" I WOULD have laughed if it weren't so strange.

He straightened up to his full six foot two and instantly dropped thirty years. When he pulled off the watch cap his red curls sprang out and he was Mike again.

"What happened?"

"A woman tried to jump," I began, and had to stop to get myself back together. "She seemed okay. And then—this is weird—you blew the horn. She looked over at you. And then she climbed over the rail. I managed to pull her back. She fought me. She wanted to step off, into nothingness—so cold—"

He pulled open the passenger door. "Get in and we'll turn the heater to blast. This baby'll do everything short of making you a hot toddy."

The imminent promise of warmth compared to the icy water of the bay . . . I shook off the thought. Illusion! I pushed away what might have happened, what could happen tomorrow, and focused on this moment, the feel of the seat, the sounds of Mike climbing in, the grind of the ignition, the blast of cold then warm air.

"I need a favor," I said.

"For you, of course." His grin implied complicity, our special connection, the way it used to be. I couldn't help but smile back, if just because

17

here was the old Mike I remembered. *For you, of course,* had been a standing joke between us so long I'd forgotten the origin.

"Drive back across the bridge again, as slow as you can."

"To see if she's there?"

"It's crazy, I know. Looking for a woman who's *not* wearing this jacket anymore."

"But it'll haunt you if you don't?"

"Yeah."

He cut underneath the freeway and back onto the roadway. Even on a clear day there's only ocean to be seen to the west, and now with the fog and dark there was nothing. He drove in the center lane while I tried to see past him, between vehicles in the three lanes on the other side. But an elephant could have been trotting down the east walkway and I'd have missed it. I wanted to check out the red jacket on my lap, but I didn't dare take my eyes off the walkway, elephant or not.

"Why the disguise?" I asked him suddenly.

"I wanted to know if you'd see through it."

"Odd timing, that."

"You'd have spotted me right off any other time. Catching your subject when they're distracted—choosing your moment's part of the disguise."

"Disguise is a two-way thing?"

"Isn't acting?"

"Yeah, but not that much. It's not like you can go into the audience seat by seat seeing who's distracted and who's not. And shooting a movie, well, you've got to be aware of what the audience will think—in the case of stunt work, what they'll assume—Damn! You sidetracked me. Steered me right into one of my favorite little sidings, stunt talk. It's one thing to do that with Mom, or John or any of the other sibs, but *me?*"

He flinched but I couldn't tell if it was a reaction to hurting me or to being found out. Later, I'd probably think back on this and be more hurt—secrets used to be things we kept from the rest of the family—but tonight it was just a minor bruise. Traffic was light by now and I could see the east walkway most of the time—the empty walkway. "So, where did you learn that?"

"Watching people."

"When were you watching people?"

He looked over at me surprised. It was such a real expression that I suddenly understood that all the others weren't. "I've always watched people. Didn't you know that? Most people don't pay that much attention. Even you." He hesitated. "You watched bodies, how they moved, but you didn't watch people. Didn't have to. I did it for both of us."

I shivered. He saw it. "Hey, if I hadn't, you would have been grounded every other day. You can't deflect questions if you don't know the questioner."

"You were the master." He had saved my tail *a lot* when I was the wild kid. It'd seemed cool—then. "But it still doesn't explain the disguise."

"What you're really asking isn't about me, it's why your jumper would put on a look-at-me jacket to hurl herself into oblivion."

Again, it wasn't my question. Again, I slid into the siding. "It makes no sense. But, okay. Why care how she looked? Who was she dressing for, the bridge cameras?"

"A lover out with someone new? Make 'im guilty. Show 'im what he lost?"

"And then jump out of despair? Very, *very* B movie."

"But she wore red. Someone less observant than you wouldn't have noticed what she had on under it."

"Which wouldn't have mattered, because she'd be dead! She wasn't planning on me pulling her back—and doing it by her jacket. She wasn't faking, Mike, she was on the other side of the railing. She'd already thrown her purse over."

"To conceal her identity?"

"Sure seems like it. Can't you go any slower?"

"Yeah, if you don't mind that van driving into our back seat."

"Let him go around."

Another time in these couple months since his return I'd've hesitated, picked my words carefully in a way that marked the difference from how we used to be. Now I peered past him and said, "Why *did* you conceal your identity?"

Mike laughed, started to speak, then seemed to reconsider. "Thing is, Darce, I don't want to be spotted, to be the focus again. I know there had to be some mention of me when I got back, after being kept in the news all those years. I had to do payback. But now—"

"What's that? Slow down!"

He pumped the brake. Behind us horns blared. "Is it—"

"No. Just the patrol cart! I don't know why I'm wasting my time when I can barely tell a cart from a woman. I should forget this and check out that jacket. Can you drive with the overhead light on?"

"Not in a convertible. Check the glove box."

Of course there was a flashlight. The car belonged to my brother Gary, and he hated to be without anything. There was also a knife, small water bottle, and what appeared to be a hatchet for a hobbit. The light was surprisingly bright. It showed the tight weave of the wool, the thickness of the gold braid, and the shine on the brass buttons. "Label says Hartoon, London. But it could've come from anywhere, right? Designer boutique? Local resale shop?"

"As opposed to her flying in from London to go off the bridge? Yeah."

"I didn't hear an accent, not that you have to be English to live there."

"Or visit and put down a credit card."

Franticness and exhaustion pulled at me. What messages could there be in what I was holding on my lap? I inhaled slowly, concentrated on feeling the breath leave, did it a couple more times till I could really see again that brief time before I grabbed her and the scuffle began. "You were driving by, you blew the horn. She turned toward, and for an instant here's what I thought, that she was like some girl who'd been carrying a torch for you all these years and suddenly there you were, beeping at her. And then she realized you weren't—not at her." I paused. "Were you?"

"No way. I was looking for you. Trying to see where you were on the bridge, gauge how long it'd be till you made it to the end. Her? I never saw her at all. Just you."

I nodded, not that he noticed. "Okay. But her—if you're on the brink of jumping off the Golden Gate Bridge, you'd've already squeezed dry every hope you had. If a horn sounded you wouldn't look up. You'd go about your business—the business of killing yourself. But she didn't." I remembered her strange parting words. "You know what she said to me? 'I did one decent thing in my life and you ruined it.'"

"*You saved her fucking life!*"

The jacket was on my lap. It was at least something concrete to deal with. I ran my fingers over the soft wool. "Funny," I said, "I wouldn't have expected it to be soft." I stretched the two small pockets that would have come at the bottom of her ribs. Empty. There was a slit pocket over the left breast, only an inch deep. "Wait, what's this? Paper." I had to pull it out between my first and second fingers. It was just a scrap of ordinary white paper—office paper—folded over and over into a narrow strip. There was nothing jotted down on it. It looked familiar in the way common things do.

"It's so little to go on. But we've got to find her. We can't let her go home, put on a different jacket, and try again."

"Very little." The old Mike would have jumped in, eager for the challenge, sure he could have made it work. But now? Now, I realized, he was considering.

"What's holding you back?" I needed to know. Otherwise, I'd have to admit to myself that this guy sitting next to me, inhabiting my brother's body, was a stranger. He was the guy who'd lived somewhere else for twenty years, not the kid I'd grown up with. "What?" I prodded.

It was a moment before he said, "Nothing. I'm in." I heard the words but could tell he still had one foot on the outside. He continued, "What've we got? Let's assume she's local, like you first figured. That narrows it to what, a million women?"

"We've got this paper," I reminded him. I unfolded it. "Wait!" I grabbed for the flashlight. "There is something on it. Or *was*. Damn, why don't people write in ink? Pull over!"

"What is it?"

"Number. Looks like phone, but it's so smudged. Two oh . . . Two eight? One? Seven? I don't—"

"I'll do it," the old Mike said.

"But there could be a hundred possible—"

"I'll work it out."

"But—"

"Hey, I've got ways. Connections. You'll have the top ten by dawn! That's when you Zen types like to get up, right?"

In spite of everything I grinned. This was old Mike! Making it work was his gift.

The first few bars of Audioslave's "I Am the Highway" played.

"Your phone?"

He glanced down. "Mom."

"Oh, wait. We can't tell her about this, not right before your birthday dinner—"

Mike had been told, by more than one of us, but there was no way he could grasp the effect of this day. He hadn't watched the stilted attempts at jollity, the cautious choice of topics unconnected to the past, us oh-so-carefully avoiding mention of the increasing time that had passed, the decreasing likelihood of his ever being found . . . alive. The type of thing the family of the woman on the bridge would have faced if she'd succeeded. But, being Mike, he'd intuited a lot and was intent on this year's celebration blotting out all the bad years.

He clicked on the phone. "Hey, Mom. What's cooking?" It was his old-time greeting, the joke being the same beef stew she always kept ready for us, our friends, and pretty much anyone any time. I could picture her smiling in a way she hadn't the whole twenty years he'd been gone. We couldn't undermine that. I glanced over and he gave me a thumbs up.

"Darcy's gotta do some Zen stuff," he said. "You know how it is, nothingness isn't nothing. She's going to drop me at the cable car—Hey, there's one coming! Heat up a big bowl for me. Bye." He pulled over and was out of the car before I could speak.

It wasn't till he was hanging on the outside of the Hyde Street car, waving, that I realized he'd bolted before I got a chance to find out how he planned to go about translating that slip of paper into a name and address.

He could tell me now. After all, all he was doing was hanging on to the cable car pole. I rang his number.

He didn't answer.

I dialed Mom. "Hi. Listen, when Mike gets there—"

"Mike's coming?"

"You just . . . Isn't he?"

"Not that I know of, honey. But if he does I'll tell him to call you. And you'll remember the rhubarb pie, right?"

"Yeah, Mom, his favorite. I'll have it there before you put the salmon on. It'll be a great day, won't it?"

"The best."

I hung up. If she hadn't called him, who had? What had they said to make him burst out from behind the wheel and run for the cable car?

4

I SLID OVER, pulled the seat a couple notches forward, and headed to North Beach to leave the car. But my driving was off, my hands grabbing hard to the wheel, and suddenly the tears I'd held threatened to burst out. It wasn't just about the woman in red, but the brother who'd just been sitting next to me.

By the time I dumped the car I was glad to double-time it down Columbus ignoring the tables of outdoor diners scarfing pizza like it was just another fine night in North Beach. Who could blame them? The scene on the bridge wasn't replaying in their heads.

I headed through the courtyard into the building. The zendo—meditation hall—on the ground floor was dark. I hurried upstairs and found Leo—Garson-roshi, the abbot—sitting cross-legged in his room, waiting for me.

Leo might have been sitting zazen there on his futon. His legs were crossed in full lotus, a position of torture for most Westerners, except for those who'd grown used to it over years of facing the wall. But he wasn't turned to the wall now. He was indicating a teapot.

I nodded, lit the burner under a pan of water, and when the bubbles almost—but not quite—danced, I poured it into the black iron pot on the tray in front of him, as I had done countless times since I'd become his assistant. The little black pot was old and rounded on the bottom and I had to hold the handle to the side and brace it just so to keep from sending the boiling water over the floor and him. It took all my concentration, which was exactly the point. Other times I'd grumbled silently, but tonight I was thankful to be pulled into this bubble of calm, doing this one small manageable task, saving one person from scalding. As he intended.

I turned off the burner, steadied the pot, and sat on a *zafu*, a black disc of a cushion, across from him. "How'd you know?"

"Your brother called."

Mike! You were looking out for me, like always. Even if—

He looked across at me. "How are you?"

In a formal Zen interview, *dokusan*, this question sparks an instant response. How are you? *Who* are you? *What* are you? What are you this very instant without past or future, just now? But this time I replied to it as the query of a friend. "I don't know."

"'Don't know' is a high state." He was answering as the Zen master. He meant not knowing is not basing your reaction on past, on future, on assumptions. Not assuming. It's about being poised to move in any direction. Not knowing is reality.

But still there was a question in his voice.

"I keep picturing her jumping. She'd've done it if I hadn't—I see her looking at me and then . . . "

"Picturing. An assumption."

I flinched, then admitted. "Yeah, pretending I know."

He poured tea into our small ceramic mugs. It was a task I, the assistant—*jisha*—should have done. It was a sign of his concern. I wanted to pick up the mug and drink down his caring, but it was too soon, the tea would scald my tongue, the mug burn my fingers. I put my hand over the cup, feeling the steam. Suddenly, everything in this small, bare room—the futon on the floor, the unpainted wood dresser, the book turned face down on the floor, the teapot, Leo in his sweatshirt and pants, the smudge of dirt on the sole of his left foot, the cool air on my neck, the grind of the bus at the corner, the scent of the tea, Leo himself—every bit of it was alive, unique, mine, too valuable to give up.

"After I pulled her back, she knocked me down hard, banged my head. Then she left her cute red jacket and vanished. Why?"

I was expecting a quote from some ancient Zen sutra. What he said was, "If you're going to disappear, best not to wear red."

Huh?

"Where are you now?"

"What?"

He sipped the hot tea, put down the cup, and said nothing. He was telling me—no, waiting for me to realize—that I wasn't operating in the now. *Now?* "All right." I took a sip of my tea, using the movement to focus, to let go of imagining and its seductions, of the theories I wanted to try out. "Now," I said, "I know nothing about her except that she left her jacket after I saved her from killing herself. I can only speculate—"

"Or not," Leo said.

Despite everything I laughed. And he smiled too.

"But if I don't speculate how am I going to find her?"

"Going down the wrong path isn't necessarily progress."

"But I've got to do *something*. I can't just let her—"

"You have a message, from Jed Elliot. Your call's at 6:00 AM."

"Yikes. I've got to get to bed. But, how can I just abandon her? I have to—"

He turned his attention to his tea and took another sip, as if to say: Words! A flurry of words!

I put down my cup and stood up. "Dammit, that's all I've got!"

He took another sip. No reproof, no response.

I knew he understood, but I was frustrated, baffled, exhausted.

He lifted the pot, poured more tea in my cup, but didn't offer me the cup. He was saying the interview wasn't over. The choice was mine.

But even now I could see past my feelings to the choice I needed to make. I sat down again.

As soon as I asked the question I realized it was the one beneath all the swirl. I said, "What is death?"

"What is life?" He finished his cup.

It wasn't, I realized, a question. It was the answer.

5

SHE'S NOT ON the bridge now. She doesn't know where she is, isn't thinking about that, isn't thinking at all. The air pings silently against her face, cold, damp, alive.

"I'm alive. Alive!" It's too stunning for speech. She rides on, feeling her feet against the pedals, the burn of freedom in her thighs. She looks up through the tall trees—Golden Gate Park!—at the dark sky. It's wonderful! She wants to ride forever in the wordless freedom.

The woman who pulled her back: How can she ever repay her? She eases off on the pedals, lets the bike roll to a stop. "I didn't even thank her! I'm alive; I'm *alive!*"

She sees the red-haired woman lying on the walkway, remembers smacking her down there. Tears burst from her eyes. She's shaking so hard she has to stop the bike. "How could I do that? She gave me my life!"

Suddenly it's vital to get back, to thank her and thank her and thank her. Frantically she looks around, trying to remember how she got here, but the moments since the stranger pulled her back over the rail have been disconnected. There is no "route to here," there's just "here."

Headlights break the fog. Police? She can't deal with police. She swings onto the bike and heads over the grass into the bushes. *Be careful. You don't know who's in there!* She laughs out loud. She should be dead—how can she worry about guys smoking hash in the bushes?

The vehicle slows, stops, starts up again. The fog sucks it in.

It's enough to break her sense of freedom. She's alive, yes, but nothing's changed. She made her deal; she still has to pay.

But not yet. She gets back on the bike and rides into the fog.

6

WHAT IS LIFE? When I sat zazen in my room before going to bed I wasn't pondering the question, but it was in the back of my mind. I went to sleep with it on my mind. But I found myself in my dream, falling, falling, waiting to hit the water, crashing into it so hard it startled me awake momentarily. Each time I jolted awake, I checked my phone. As if its ring wouldn't have woken me! It was too early for Mike's call, but that didn't deter me the next time I woke. Never have I been so grateful for the alarm at five in the morning. I was sweating and freezing and very glad for the 6:00 AM call. Late as it was, I had only ten minutes for zazen—like peering into a familiar room you can't take a seat in—but I was thankful for that focus on reality.

When I got to the set at the high point of Dolores Street—another location I had scouted—I stopped at the lunch wagon to pick up coffee and eye my phone again, as if to conjure up his message.

With its wide grassy center divider of glorious tall, fat palm trees and its lovingly restored Victorians and Edwardians, Dolores Street is all San Francisco. The original white stucco mission church there, built in 1776, still stands open to the public, with its tiny graveyard peopled by the Miwok, Spanish, and Irish dead of long ago. Three blocks east, Mission Street is still the heart of the city's traditional Hispanic neighborhood. I'd suggested it to Jed Elliot, the second unit director, talked up its crowded sidewalks, dotted by taquerias and women in bright flow-ered print skirts grilling tacos to sell from their carts—ones we could mock up and send flying in the car gag. I'd carried on about the old bars with signs above the door: OPEN AT 6:00 AM, and ones in the window: LADIES WELCOME.

I'd weighed the local color against the amount of traffic and the hassle of getting the city to block it off, and also dangers like light posts I might hit and end up hiking the company's insurance. And then there were the un-avoidable bursts of noise from customers at those stands, laundromats and early opening-time bars. With delivery trucks sure to try sneaking through the roadblocks, the potential for interruptions was impressive. But in the interval between my eyeballing the site, then contacting the city and start-ing the search for each of the property owners likely to be involved, our main backer'd gone belly-up.

Still, I'd called the city liaison to stall, figuring to keep the faith with a project I tried not to believe was headed nowhere. When suddenly, a new group of backers leapt up—not as reliable as the first guy, but with a con-nection to a big money couple in the city—and the word again was Go. But we had to be gone by Thursday, i.e., three short days from now.

Oh, and our block of Mission had been nabbed for a church fair.

Then I'd spotted the peak of the hill at Dolores and 21st. I'd pictured myself driving up, hitting the turn so fast it'd look as if I was about to roll the car—not just over but all the way down to 24th Street.

Who could not be hooked?

Here, blocking off the incoming streets wasn't a problem. But waking the neighbors sure was. We'd had to drive the trucks in before dark and park them overnight, blocking the wheels for some of them on the steep streets. Plus, we'd hired a couple of off-duty cops, not only for fear of our trucks being ripped off by one of the pro gangs and halfway to L.A. by now, but to keep amateur boosters from clanking and smashing and waking the neighbors, thus making our next request for a permit lots harder. It'd been such a hassle I half-wished I'd just hunted up Declan Serrano at the cop shop and paid off. But we had an arrangement with the city, one I wasn't about to screw up by aligning myself with the boss of the Mission district (and beyond).

Even so, rerouting traffic doesn't make you—much less the city—popular with the citizenry. We had an hour, two at best, to block out the action before police would close us down. Tomorrow we'd do the take. As I crossed the barricade, I couldn't help but smile to finally see the crane and dolly in place and the old Honda sitting ready for its moment of stardom.

Thoughts—*just thoughts!* as Leo would remind me—of the woman on the bridge kept tugging. I was glad to have the necessity of the now to push them aside.

Jed Elliot, my favorite second unit director, was running this stunt operation. His normal mode was three double-caffs tight: Mr. Perfectionism. That's what you want from the person responsible for the final word on the safety of the movie stunts. He was used to giving orders and having young assistants jump. But now he was snout-to-snout with a fellow I'd never seen. Jed had faced down the city liaison and screamed at a first unit director who could've fired him, but this guy had him on his heels. Compared to this lunatic Jed was Mr. Calm. This guy was bouncing foot to foot, arms flying, head in Jed's face as if there was any chance of Jed or anyone else in the Mission failing to hear his low opinion of Jed's operating plan, personnel choices, and all-around competence, as illustrated by the ranter's not having been notified of today's set-up here.

There was no way Jed could stop the guy. At six in the morning! At this site I'd busted my butt to set up!

Only money could create such a scene. Was he one of the new backers?

It didn't matter who he was, because in a minute, blinds in Victorians were going to snap up, neighbors were going to glare, and we'd be toast.

I could not let that happen, backer or no.

I strode over. "Hey, Jed. That the car?"

"What? Yeah." Quickly, he added, "You met Macomber Dale?"

"Mac," he snapped. Seizing the moment, Jed moved off.

"Darcy Lott."

"*You're* the stunt driver?"

"I am. And you're—"

"The producer."

The producer! Big leap from backer to *the* producer. Was that truth or self-promotion? I'd have to find out, pronto.

For the moment, I flashed a smile at the newborn producer, gave his hand a squeeze and release, and called to Jed. "How're we on time?"

"You can finish your coffee and do the check, both."

This time my smile was genuine. With a stunt car, particularly one I'm going to be close to rolling at the top of the hill, checking it out involves a lot more than lifting the hood.

I nodded a "so long" to Macomber. For all the good it did.

He kept pace with me.

I picked up speed but the hint was lost on him. I'd intended to rescue Jed, but at this rate I'd soon be screaming myself. I put my cup on the car roof and turned.

He looked at me challengingly. "I know cars. I have an old Studebaker I rebuilt from—"

"Hey!" I'm not at my most gracious at this hour of the morning.

"I can—"

I took a breath and gave him an easy exit. "Go away or I'll run you over. It'll make a great shot."

"Listen, I'm not some gofer here. Practically, this whole movie's coming out of my pocket. I can—"

"No, you can't! If you're planning to hang over my shoulder, you can't. You *can* force Jed to waste time hunting up another driver, but you're not going to get anyone as good, and all that time you'll be paying all these people, plus the city—out of your pocket. Or—" The set had come to a standstill. Everyone, including Jed, was gawking—"you can leave me to do my job. Your choice." I needed to let him save face. I needed to calm things—

But I wasn't calming things. I was glaring at the guy, virtually snarling, "Your investment."

"Yeah, *my* investment! Hey, Elliot, why you got all these jokers standing around like it's free entertainment time here." He glowered. Jed was staring, shocked at my outburst. So was I. Now all I could do was to shut my mouth.

The car was a Honda, an old model I knew pretty well. I'd be riding the slide at the corner, throwing a 90, a seriously tarted-up left-hand turn. I lifted the hood, and stared down while I felt the throbbing in my chest, the clenching in my neck and shoulders, as I made myself stop and focus on them. There's no upside to pissing off the producer. Sets him out to get you, puts the rest of the crew on edge, and gives the director second thoughts about hiring you again. For me, with ambitions to be second unit director myself, I'd basically screwed myself. If, that is, this guy was more than a blowhard.

I checked the tires, the suspension, got in, and started the engine. All good. I shifted into first, let out the clutch. This was only the prep, though. Tomorrow I'd be gunning it, shifting to second, ramming the emergency brake to create the skid and squeal, then giving the wheel a slight pull to create the 90. Spin it too hard—easy to do—and I'd find myself in a full 180 shooting back down Dolores on the wrong side of the street.

But I wouldn't spin too hard. It was a simple, basic gag. Driving a low, wide Honda Civic's like riding a frog.

I circled the block, feeling the gear knob in my palm, sensing the point when the clutch released, seeing how fast I could take a corner without squealing. By the time I eased back to the start mark I felt like myself again.

Macomber Dale pulled open the passenger door and plopped himself in, primed for battle.

I just laughed. "What're you doing?"

"Auditing my investment."

"Good you're sitting, 'cause you're going to be bored to death."

"Oh, no, not me."

Outside the camera crew was adjusting the tracks for the dolly camera that would parallel the action. My first run would be almost slo-mo, that camera chugging beside me. There was another on the sidewalk near the corner hidden behind a plant and an overhead at the corner to get the spin, plus one mounted on the dashboard giving the driver's-eye view. After those were in the can we'd set up the speed shot, cameras in place to catch the car vrooming around the corner, smacking a flower or taco or fruit stand and screeching off. The whole sequence would be woven into shots of the actress in the driver's seat pretending to drive her unmoving car.

I turned off the engine.

Dale shot me a look. "What're you doing?"

"Waiting."

"Why?"

"That's what movie making is. For me. You, you can leave any time."

But he didn't. He settled back against the window and said, "So, just how long've you been a stunt girl?"

I filed away the "girl." "Professionally? Since college."

"You been doing car tricks all that time?"

Car tricks? Girl? Did the guy think I'd never been goaded? Me, with three older brothers? Me, who'd spent twenty years in a testosterone job. I wasn't going to lose it again. Let him try. "I've done this, high falls, burn work. You have to have the whole package."

"Just what is your package?"

The camera slid back three yards and Jed signaled me forward. Except for momentary glee at the end of a saved gag, he always looked like a desiccated lemon worried about life on the compost heap. But now he seemed more unnerved than normal and the cause of that distress was Macomber here in the car with me. Jed was hoping for peace, hoping I'd get that. I did.

I eased off the clutch so smoothly we were halfway there before we felt the car moving.

"How's this baby been modified?"

"Shop in Berkeley."

He started to reply and caught himself.

"You done driving like in *Matrix*? You pancaked cars?"

The camera on the dolly slid forward. I peered around the dashboard mount that would give the driver's-eye view, and followed.

"How many bones you break?"

Where did this guy come from? He was like ultimate groupie meets Mr. Snide! Money was tight, but . . .

Money was tight. I played the clutch against the gas and inched forward.

"How many times—"

"Macomber—"

"Mac. It's Mac. And don't tell me to stop with the questions. People've been saying that all my life—"

"Slow learner?"

"Want to know why? 'Cause I got questions. That's how come I'm where I am and—"

"My turn. You ready to answer?"

"Fire away."

I turned to him. If he'd been a dog he'd've been one of those little yappers. But he wouldn't have been bad looking if he'd ever been still enough to judge. Dark brown eyes, black hair cut short, obligatory jeans and black T-shirt, three of those colored bracelets for charity. His fingers were on the dashboard camera. In a minute he'd be messing with the lens.

I said, "Have you ever tried suicide?" It just came out.

For an instant he was still. "No."

"You're lying, aren't you?"

"No."

"But you've considered it."

"Hell, who hasn't? I bet you have, haven't you? Am I right?"

"I'll tell you if you answer me this."

He gave a sharp nod.

"What is life?"

"Huh?"

"You decided you didn't want to die. What is it you don't want to give up? What is 'life'?"

"What kind of question—"

"This is how stunt doubles talk while we're waiting." *As if!* "So?" I'd asked to unnerve him, with luck to get rid of him. But now I was curious what he'd say.

He started to speak but didn't. He felt for the lever and pushed the seat back. He glanced at the door, reached for the handle, and hesitated. He was wavering between options, both of which were going to reduce him in my mind and maybe his own. If he could come up with a good exit line, he'd be home free. But that kind of thing, either you've got it or you don't. There's no crafting it.

Clearly, he was in the *don't* column.

His eyes had drawn back as if into a picture he didn't want to see. He looked like ending his life was a reasonable option. My question had been serious, but I'd never intended this grim a reaction. He said, "Life? It's better than death. At least with life you know what you've got."

"The devil you know? That's all?"

"Yeah. Now you? When did you think about suicide?"

He hadn't answered me, not really, but I hadn't expected him to. What he had done was stop jerking around. That was worth an answer. "At the end of college."

"Why didn't you do it?"

"I wanted to go to New Orleans first. I figured that meant I wasn't real serious."

"You're lying."

"You don't know the lure of the Big Easy. I went as soon as I graduated, had the time of my life."

"I still say you're lying."

Suddenly, I felt bad about my not-exactly-truth. "I came upon a jumper on the bridge yesterday and pulled her back."

"So that's it?"

I couldn't tell what he meant by that. But I didn't have time to worry about it. The cameraman signaled. I was twenty feet from the corner. I checked the street. All clear. Tomorrow there'd be a mocked-up wagon on the cross street. Today there was a big cardboard X. I hit the gas, made speed, punched the emergency brake, and pulled the wheel a quarter turn to the left. The car screeched into a controlled skid, the bread and butter of stunt drivers. We spun wide at the corner. Tomorrow I'd make the brake squeal loud enough to wake the dead. Right before I was headed onto the cross street I let out the brake. The tires caught. I gave the wheel a flutter, knocked down the X, and pulled up.

Before it came to a stop, Mac leaned and hit the horn. He shot me a gotcha grin.

"Stop! What're you—" I shoved him into the door. He bounced against it, hit the horn again.

"Are you crazy?"

"Yeah! So?" He flung open the door, stumbled out, and stalked off the set.

The entire crew stood dead still, staring.

My phone vibrated.

I hesitated. Jed was charging after him. The phone shivered again.

Suddenly Jed was on his own phone. Dale kept on moving around the corner and was gone. With huge relief I pulled out my cell. The voicemail came from a number I didn't recognize, but the voice I sure did.

Mike. "Two possibles. One's a resale shop in the Women's Building on 17th. But the other is L Young on Filbert." He paused and for a moment I thought he was gone. But he added the Filbert address and cross street.

Since he'd been back, it'd been a thrill just to hear his voice. But this time I wished he'd shown up here in person, with a car. It was after seven o'clock. If she was a government employee, L Young could be leaving for work any minute. If her job was at the stock exchange she was already there. Would I have to wait till evening to find out? Evening, when she could be back on the bridge?

7

FILBERT WAS ACROSS town. I needed to think about how I was going to get there. But now, suddenly, there was plenty to occupy me in this second run-through of the gag.

Jed had managed to convince the police rep to extend our permit time. But the negotiations took a *kalpa*—in Sanskrit, the time during which water might, drop by drop, reduce Mt. Everest to Lake Everest—and though I didn't see money changing hands, I heard the name Declan Serrano mentioned. I knew he did nothing for free.

Meanwhile, everything that had not gone wrong on the first run now began to. The drive on the camera cart locked. The light shifted, bounced off a shiny metal sign into my eyes and, more importantly, into the dashboard lens. It took a minor *kalpa* to roust the building owner and get the sign covered. And so on. By the time we finished it was almost nine o'clock and the chances of finding L Young at home had plummeted. Still, you don't try to kill yourself and trot into work the next morning. With luck, she was in bed, still stunned by her close call with death.

Right after Mike disappeared, twenty years ago when I was in high school, food lost any flavor, every step was a trudge, and any word of comfort an intrusion. I'd never made a suicide plan, but Macomber Dale was right—I'd thought about it.

Now, for the first time, I wondered if my brothers and sisters, if Mom herself, had had that seductive urge to just end the pain of missing him, of picturing him dead—of wondering what they might have done to cause it.

"Darcy!"

When I looked up, Jed was almost at the window. "The city shut us down!"

"I thought we had a permit?"

"We did—until you leaned on the horn and woke up the neighborhood. How many calls d'you think it takes to the cops—"

"Hey, wait! That wasn't me hitting the horn. That was that ass Macomber Dale."

"But you—"

"Me nothing!"

"You—"

"Stop! Just stop it now. Just—" I was inhaling, focusing on it for the length of that breath. If I were the second unit director—"Who the hell is Macomber Dale anyway? And why are we stuck with him on the set?"

Jed looked about to snap at me, then he just sighed. "He's . . . what he seems—a loose cannon. He's been on the fringes for years trying to get a foothold in production."

"I can see why he failed, but how come we—?"

"He got enough money from Aaron Adamé's wife—"

"Oh." No need to ask if that mover-and-shaker loot was what was keeping us afloat. "So, then, what do we need to pay—*give*—Serrano?"

"Zip. If it was just one call, he could ignore it. A couple, he could drag out the response till the weekend. But not the whole fucking neighborhood."

"He can do what he wants; that's what I've heard."

"He doesn't want. It's already been a big hassle; makes him look bad in the neighborhood and downtown, too. We're not getting any favors from him, now, thanks to you—thanks to the horn. You know if you'd—"

"Yeah well I didn't, and neither did you. The next time you see that jerk you can tell him he's screwing us. What about Berkeley?"

Jed stared. "Berkeley?"

"The marina. We could do this scene there."

"And redo half the story line?"

I took another deep breath. And in that time I missed my turn in the argument.

Jed was so into the flow he picked up the other side. "We haven't shot the lead up. It'd take some adjusting, but it's not impossible."

"This week? Just the negotiations—"

"But if we're clear and crisp on the parameters—"

"We don't have parameters."

"We can get them." He paused. "*You* can get them. I'll call you with the contact in Berkeley. Get me the stats today."

Today!

"By three. I don't want to be calling over there when the only people picking up the phone are on their way home."

Impossible! I stuck out my hand and said, "Done." Stunt work was scarce and getting more so. No way could I blow off this job, or Jed Elliot, not if I ever planned to be stunt coordinator.

In less than an hour Macomber Dale had managed to piss off everyone on the set, residents all around, and the main cop in the Mission district. Amazing.

As for me, I was livid and, at the same time, desperate to get to Filbert and talk to L Young. Still, I could scoot over the bridge now and scope out the site enough for the paperwork. I'd lived in Berkeley all through college. I knew the marina. It'd be less than two hours before I swung back by Filbert Street. Two hours really wouldn't make any difference, I told myself, and I could not just ignore my job. *Why do you even care about her now?* my oldest brother'd demand. *You saved her, isn't that enough? Let it go!*

But I couldn't, not yet, anyway. I couldn't even explain why. But it didn't matter because soon I'd be face to face with her—or at least someone she'd intended to phone—and, maybe, I'd see that she was okay.

"Okay, I'm off," I said to Jed.

"Not so fast. Nellen needs to do some work on the car." He nodded at the camera crew guy over by the lunch wagon.

"How long?"

"Hour, he says."

I didn't bother to ask what that meant in real time. Filbert now; Berkeley Marina after.

I passed Nellen the key and the garage location, snagged a donut from the lunch wagon, considered another coffee and, sadly, admitted that the point of no return had already come. Normally, I'd've bemoaned the rest of the day spent in the bland and arid land of no coffee, but right now I didn't have time.

Cabs do exist in San Francisco, but you wouldn't know it unless you're at a hotel. I turned to Nellen. "Did you drive here?"

A couple minutes later I was saying I owed him, sliding into his Jeep Cherokee, and thinking luck was with me.

It was. Crosstown traffic was light and, miracle of all miracles, I found a parking spot on Filbert. Better yet, the address was not one of those apartment buildings set up to keep out strangers, but a duplex with doors at the top of the stairs and L Young's name big as life on the mail slot. I hesitated a moment, trying to tamp down my hopes, to ignore the fear that she'd be gone, on her way to carry out her threat, then braced myself and pushed the bell. It wasn't just a question of whether she was home. After all, L Young could be a man—a single initial in the listing often meant that—or—

But she wasn't. Louise Young was a middle-aged African American woman in her bathrobe, a woman who eyed me, realized I was not the UPS driver, and was disappointed.

Nowhere near as crushed as I was. Before she could close the door I said, "Do you have a roommate? I'm looking for a white woman about my height, dark hair, chin-length, thin. She bikes. She—"

"I wish I had time for friends."

"She had your phone number. Are you a therapist or—"

"I've got a one-year-old and a three-year-old. They *are* my work." A screech came from inside. She shot a glance back. "Your friend could be next door and I wouldn't notice her. Sorry." She shut the door.

I walked back to the Jeep, got in, and slammed the door. A full hour wasted and I was no closer to my jumper. I—

"Don't complain!" Leo once told me that, not as a chide but as an instruction. His intention hadn't been merely to save my companion from a rant or a whine—he'd meant: Don't complain in your mind. Don't underwrite illusion.

So, I focused on getting the vehicle back to Nellen before he finished with the Honda I'd be taking to Berkeley.

But the Honda wasn't ready.

This was turning into one helluva day—a day that made not complaining a challenge.

Without much hope I headed on foot for the resale shop.

The Women's Building is a hundred-year-old Mission Revival–style former gymnasium, built by German exercise enthusiasts. It boasts rounded windows, great, colorful murals on the exterior walls, and rental space in-side. Women Re-entering was on the ground floor.

Inside two women were sorting clothes. Me, I love secondhand shops. Each one has its own style. My preference is vintage, theatrical, or just weird. But this one looked more conservative—good clothes, the kind worn by the steadily employed.

"We're closed. Unless you're donating." A large blond woman in a sweatshirt she couldn't have given away even here nodded toward a table.

Women Re-entering! Now I remembered hearing about this place. "So you help women prepare for job interviews?"

"And jobs. Gotta wear something to work before the first check, you know. No one thinks of that."

"Looks like you did."

"Times like these, it's tough. Thought we might . . . but no. That's a nice jacket."

My standby black jacket. I laughed. "Lucky, huh? What do you do—guilt people on the street?"

"We get the word out. You don't work in this neighborhood or you'd know. You'd be planning to give us that jacket. You're wearing it with jeans—worn jeans. It's not your only jacket, like it will be to the woman who gets it. Other people've given a lot more."

"Really? Recently? Like this week? Did a woman about my size give you a lot this week?" My jumper went to the trouble of writing down their phone number! Why else would she do that?

The blond woman looked at me quizzically.

"I'm taking that as a yes."

"Okay. A big honking yes. See that table, one woman gave us the whole lot."

I started toward it.

"Hey, what d'you think you're doing?" She all but tackled me.

"I'm not trying to take it. I just need to find her."

"You can't root through her stuff. There's a reason women want to give us their clothes and it's not because we let strangers go through their pockets. You ever give us anything? Would you if you thought someone off the street would be pawing through it to see if you'd forgotten a credit card receipt, a note from a lover who's maybe not your husband, a—"

"Whoa! I get your point. But look, I'm not nosing into her private life; I'm trying to find her."

"I don't—"

"It could be a matter of life and death."

"Could be? Is it?"

I hesitated. "I can't take the chance of it not being." For the first time she seemed unsure. I said, "Tell me her name."

Still, she didn't commit.

I unbuttoned my jacket.

She grinned, put out a hand for it, and said, "Tessa."

"Tessa what?"

"We don't require last names here. She didn't care about the tax receipt, so no need. Anyway, you're not going to find her. She gave us the clothes because she was leaving town."

I eyed the pile. "Looks like her whole closet."

"That's what she said; said she had nothing but the clothes on her back."

"Which were?"

"I don't know. Nothing that stood out."

"White T-shirt and black slacks?"

"Don't remember."

"Red jacket?"

"Not a chance."

I slipped off my own jacket. "Tell whoever gets this that it may not look like much but it's my good luck garment. I got my first job back in town wearing it."

The woman smiled. "You know, most people come in here with a bag or two. They're concerned about a tax write-off or they're not. They're happy to help, or just glad to dump. But she looked at that brown dress over there, like she was dropping a puppy at the pound. She held on to it so long I said—and this isn't like me—I said, 'We'll still be here next week. You've got time to think it over.' She said no, she didn't. But she was still holding it. Then she said, 'I was wearing it at the happiest moment of my life.'"

"Surely you asked . . . "

"I make it my business not to pry."

"But this time?"

"Well, yeah, okay. I could tell she wanted to tell me or I wouldn't have pried, you understand."

Thank God! "And?"

"What she said didn't make sense. Except to her. I mean, that dress, it's nothing special, right? It's a wear-to-work-on-Wednesday kind of dress, right? But something happened that Wednesday—"

"When?"

"Last week, maybe the week before? Meaning, recently. Something happened in that dress. What she said was that up till the call she never really believed it would happen. Then she smiled the way you do walking down the aisle, put down the dress, and left."

"Do you have any idea—"

"None. Look, I hear so many hard stories, I'm just happy to have a moment like that. More power to her wherever she is."

"Which is where?"

"Dunno."

"Didn't she give you some clue? Mention the street she lived on? Her job? Something?"

"No. Like I said, I don't pry. Don't want to know."

"It's important. Life and death, really. She had your phone number in her pocket. Do you remember a call?"

She shook her head. "The phone's just for giving out information. We keep the phone ringer off. Don't take messages. You call here, you get our address, our hours, if we need one type of garment, like winter coats. That's it. But listen, I hope you find her. I really do."

I gave her my card. "If you see her, call me." That was all I could do.

I walked out onto the sidewalk, so distracted, so frustrated I nearly smacked into a guy pushing a cart. She was gone, my jumper. My only "clue" and it'd turned out to be nothing. Now I was never going to find her. A first name is nothing. Tracking down this phone number was nothing. Why did she even write it down, much less fold up the paper to almost a toothpick and make the number halfway impossible to read?

I turned west on 18th Street, back toward the set. I'd had a temp job a block over a couple months ago.

Did she actually use it as a sort of toothpick? A wedge, maybe? Because the paper was stiffer than normal.

The paper!

I grabbed my phone. "Mike, the paper!" I wished I had it in my hand now. But I could see it in my mind: white with pale blue lines, stiffer than normal but not thicker. "You know what it could be? It's a pay slip—the part you tear off from your check. Like the ones from PayRite."

"What makes you think—"

"Stunt gigs don't pop up every day. Temp work does, or mostly. I've answered phones, typed, filed, clerked, and occasionally even waited tables.

A lot of businesses contract out their payroll, even if it's only one or two people on staff. Gary does it for his law office. They don't want to spend time thinking about tax deductions, much less worry about IRS forms."

"So? Where does that get us?"

"Is there any number on it? Employee number?"

"Two eight seven one five."

"Too long. No small company has that many workers. It'd have to be the employer number. Thanks. Later." I hung up, pulled up a number for PayRite, and called. I'd taken a lot of no's for answers this morning but I wasn't about to now.

"PayRite."

"Customer records, please." When I got a woman there, I said, "I'm customer number two eight seven one five. I think you've got our address wrong. We're having a problem—Well, just tell me what address you're using for us."

She put me on hold before coming back with: "Forty Cunningham."

"Thanks, you've been a big help," I said. A big, but not total help. Now the question was, where was Cunningham? But that's what smart-phones are for.

Hoping Nellen would have the Honda ready to go, I headed back to Dolores, where the crew would be packing away the last of our props and markers, the detritus of all our wasted work on the set.

I was a block away when a horn honked.

Macomber Dale, in a black Mercedes convertible, pulled to the curb.

8

WAVES BREAK, ROLL to shore. Cold, so cold. Is this what it is to be dead?

But she's not dead. She remembers, now, the night: peddling, coasting, riding till she was too tired to go on, ending up out here beyond the Great Highway at the edge of the Pacific. Trying to dig a cave in the dune. Too tired. Sleeping against the front wheel. Cold then, but so very tired. And yet, alive! Her skin tingles. Alive!

The thick layers of fog are less dark—morning.

It's different from last night. No euphoria now. Cold. Shivering cold.

What to do? She reaches into her pocket, pulls out a torn tissue. No money.

Nothing's changed. She should ride back to the bridge now, before— but it's already too late to beat the morning joggers. She'd climb over the rail and just get pulled back every hour like one of those bobbing birds on a cocktail glass. She starts to laugh, picturing it.

Hungry. Her stomach pushes in on itself and she sits, feeling that emptiness, feeling the cold, *feeling*.

Tonight she'll go back to the bridge. But not now. Not yet. She'll go back if she can make herself.

She has to. If there were any other way . . .

There isn't. She's been through it a hundred times. She made her choice. This is how it has to be.

She could have jumped last night. Then, it was just leaving the bike and climbing over the railing. But now everything on the ride back there will be linked to the rail. The whole trip across the bridge will be part of it. Tonight, it'll be so much harder. If there were just another way—

She can't go home. She can't even buy food. She can ride in the fog, or ride inland in the sun.

But, she sits. She watches the waves ease in, break into lace, to froth. Whoops! They're yanked back out. The process is so much more intricate, fascinating than she'd ever noticed. She doesn't mind the cold or the hunger, she is so grateful to be here. To sit here, like a clump of beach grass. To be.

Maybe she really is beyond the Great Highway. The world thinks she's dead. The only person on earth who knows she didn't is that woman, and she has no idea of her name. She *could* be dead. Everything's set up for it. Tessa Jurovik could be no more.

Death has been described as stepping through a door. The door closed on Tessa Jurovik, and now, it's opening to the new room, the new life, a new woman. A free woman. No food, no money, no place to stay. Free!

She feels the lump in her pocket, pulls out a slim cell phone, and laughs. The last connection. *Bad connection.* But this is one connection that'll be easy to break. It wasn't even her phone, not till the last couple days anyway. She walks toward the water. The water arcs and crashes, not in big waves here, but hard, so much harder than it seemed when she looked down from the bridge. She remembers the chocolate-colored water, how warm and soft it looked from up there. A shiver shoots through her. She could never face that again.

But she doesn't have to. She shifts the phone in her hand, ready to throw it into the water and be free for good.

There's a message.

Here she is at the pivotal moment in her life, her new life, and there's a phone message!

Bye, bye, message! She arcs her arm back.

It's not even her phone.

She inhales the briny air and readjusts her arm.

It's stupid, irresponsible, not to check the message. But she can't bear to undercut her freedom. She's afraid—

She's afraid.

Afraid to read it, afraid to throw the phone away. She hates it for robbing her of the wonder of just being. But she can't bring herself to toss it into the water. She's not that brave. She shoves it back in her pocket and plunks down on the sand.

But the magic's gone and in a minute she's pushing the bike toward the street, thinking about where to find food.

9

IN A PLACE known for wind and fog, what were the odds of being shadowed by two open convertibles two days in a row?

Dale leaned across a passenger seat and opened the door. The man was fighting to hide a gotcha grin. What was with this guy? He'd wrecked the entire shoot! Fine if he wanted to apologize to me, but Jed was the one he ought to be falling all over himself mea culping to. Did I want to waste any more time on him? Not likely.

"Hey," he called out, "I want to make you a proposition."

"Excuse me?"

"I want you to teach me to stunt drive."

"What?"

"You're good enough."

"Are you out of your mind? You got us booted off the site!"

"Me?"

I propped my hand on the passenger door and leaned in toward him, so he wouldn't miss a word. "Because of you the whole neighborhood was up on the horn to the cops! You cost us all the time I spent searching for the site, plus this morning, plus the time it's going to take me to scope out the Berkeley Marina and deal with the city there. Plus—"

"I'll pay you three times what you get—"

"Don't you hear—"

"Okay, twenty."

I just stared. Money guys sure live in a different world. Me, I work for six hundred dollars a day flat, plus adjustment for the specific gag. Hell, say a thou. "You're offering me twenty thousand dollars a day to teach you to drive?"

"To stunt drive."

"By which you mean?"

"Teach me to do the stunt we just set up."

"You want to do it in the final shot? So your name's in the credit roll?" *The credits of the production you've already sabotaged!* "That what you mean?"

He shrugged.

In Zen, the three poisons are greed, hate, and delusion. I didn't hate my current situation, but I wasn't deluding myself that one day soon I might not start to. With twenty thou, though, I wouldn't be taking the bus or cadging wheels from my brother. With twenty thou, I wouldn't be dressing myself out of consignment shops. With twenty thou, Mom and Mike and I would be in Waikiki in January. No wonder greed has maintained its popularity.

On the other hand, Dale was part of our production not due to his own merit but because of his money connection. This offer could be big-time delusion. "Much as I'm tempted, there's no way a novice could be ready to take over this gag by tomorrow. And even if you were the best wheelman in the city, Jed would never take the chance."

"I'm the producer."

"But you're not God." I paused, in case he needed time to process that. It's a distinction some money guys miss. "This isn't the only production Jed's ever going to work on. He's got a reputation to maintain in this city, and not as good a one today as he had yesterday. He won't endanger the crew, bystanders, property, not to mention his relationship with the director—"

"But I—"

"Let's say you graze a fire hydrant. Say it breaks. It gushes all over the street, causes a mega traffic tie up, is the lead story on the nightly news. The city film commission takes a hit, the mayor gets flack, they chew out Declan Serrano, and Jed Elliot'll be lucky to be directing the second unit in a high school play in Hollister. If there was such a gig."

"But—"

"Mac, I can tell you're not a guy used to taking no for an answer, but— I'm sorry—no way." I wasn't sorry, but come the cold rains of January I might well be.

He went still. Then, suddenly, he burst back to life with a fury. "I'll work it out with Jed. Then, you'll be on board, right?"

"Sure. Whatever Jed okays, I'll go along with it." *Like that was going to happen.* Jed was nothing if not cautious.

"I'll call you. Keep your time free."

"I'll sit by the phone. In the meantime, let's see how you drive. Drop me at Cunningham Alley. Follow my directions." That'd be a first for him!

How he drove surprised me. He looked both ways before exiting the alley onto 21st Street, checked for pedestrians before turning left onto Valencia, and hung a U two blocks later where it was legal. He pulled into the alley and parked.

Definitely not what I'd expected.

"Thanks." I got out.

He reached for his door.

I put a hand on his arm. "Bye."

"I've got time."

"I don't. Bye." And I was out.

Twenty thousand dollars had appeared and vanished and it still wasn't ten in the morning.

On one side of the street was a playground, on the other five cottages, four kept up and the last—number 40—only escaped being neglected because there was nothing to neglect. All decorative trim had been removed and the siding modernized past any individuality. The paint was the kind of beige they use on public park buildings and the stoop held not so much as a doormat. Even the "40" had been painted beige. But it was there and I rang the bell.

10

IT'S AN ABANDONED breakfast burrito. Before—*before*—she'd have felt queasy just picking up the half-gobbled glob to toss it in the trash. Now she doesn't even bother eating from the other end. The pinto beans are still warm, the cheese still gooey, and the salsa not gringo pale. Yesterday she'd have quipped that it looked like this was going to be its second trip through a digestive tract. Now she doesn't even pause to smile at that, nor to savor every bite. She's too hungry to stop wolfing.

She's in a wide alley that passes for a courtyard between a Mom-and-Pop store and an electronic repair shop. Minutes ago bike messengers lounged against the grocery wall, next to their wheels, eating, grumbling, laughing. She used all her patience hanging out a block away till she saw the whole gang of messengers take off, flying downtown to circle around, ready to swoop in on the first emergency pick-up. They're an odd, splinter group, choosing to start out this far away from most of their business. But it means when they go, they're gone for the day, and now the place is hers. She's just lucky the guy with the burrito didn't beg his buddies for another two minutes to finish. The phone is virtually burning a hole in her pocket, but the wind is blowing free and she's still high from the ride up here.

The block's empty now. Wind would be whipping leaves if there were any trees. In the repair shop window a TV flickers. It's turned to Channel 4, the local station that lost its network affiliation and is now heavy on news, reruns, and infomercials. She watches a piece about a neighborhood garden somewhere in the East Bay, without sound, which doesn't matter because she neither cares about gardening nor the East Bay. What she cares about is putting off dealing with the phone.

Sighing, she pulls it out. How bad can the message be? It's not even her phone. Maybe it's been there for days. In any case, no one's going to be calling her.

She glances back at the screen, as if for comfort from a friend, but the anchor's now interviewing a man in front of an official-looking building somewhere.

Before she can come up with another excuse she clicks the phone. Text: From: United Airlines

Dear Tessa Jurovik: We regret UAL#212, SFO to Miami canceled. We will hold a seat on UAL#422, Oak to Miami lv. 5:04; 1 passenger, pls confirm by 4:04.

Yesterday at 5:04 PM! She remembers a digital weather/time sign outside a bank announcing 5:05, telling her she was too early for the bridge, that she had to kill a quarter of an hour. She—that woman yesterday—was annoyed, like her bus was late. She had an important appointment. She wanted to go deal.

She laughs. "No wonder I didn't jump; I was flying to Miami!"

Life, it gets stranger and stranger. She slides her back down the wall, squat-sitting there opposite the repair shop window. The anchor—

Suddenly she connects this day to the flow of days that stopped for her last night. It's the day of the award ceremony, the one she never expected to see. It'll be at ten o'clock, and the video will be on Channel 4, at the end of the hour, the feel-good story time. She can't believe she's actually going to see it, sitting here watching the clip. She's smiling so widely she can feel the wind on her teeth. She could float off into the clouds.

Life is indeed strange.

11

DALE HAD TO back-and-forth three times before he could drive out of the alley. I gave him points for resisting the temptation to back out into traffic. The whole process was long enough and loud enough that it took me only one light knock to bring a woman to the door of the converted house that was number 40.

She was maybe twenty, bone thin, with long dark hair knotted at the nape and a tattoo of a dancing Shiva rising from her chest and reaching some of his many arms across her shoulders. Several more arms shot up the sides of her neck in a way that was at once stunning and frightening. A needle that close to the carotid!

"Tessa—" I began after introductions.

But a screeching kettle grabbed Kristi's attention. She nodded me in, raced across the room, and doused a teabag. The concoction smelled like cardamom and manure.

The place itself was not an office but a workroom with a smattering of papers, the kind that might be used in collages, two copy machines, each on a long fake wood table, a tiny fridge, and an industrial sink that suggested this room had originally been a basement. The only decoration was, in fact, a collage, one that looked much better than this space deserved. In contrast were the windows. They might have looked out over the basketball courts across the street to the south or the jungle gym to the west, except that they'd been painted white six feet high. "So they don't look in, or you don't look out?"

She took that as a comment rather than a question.

"What is this place?"

She was plugging in the space heater. "Skilled Copy."

"You duplicate skills?"

She shot a look that acknowledged the joke without appreciating it. "We make copies, skillfully. Like for lawyers when they've got eight things to send to twenty people but some of those people only get the first and third thing, some the last two, some get the cover letter, and one gets the originals and all the copies plus copies of all the cover letters. And the client wants a copy of everything everyone got. And it's all got to be in the mail by five, with those little green 'certified' slips."

"Got it." I glanced around. "What're you copying now?"

"Nada. We never have orders waiting. It's all last minute. If a client's prepared days ahead, they can handle it in their own office. If they're calling here, it's a crisis. There've been times we had to work like crazy till the last second and then just about kill ourselves to make it to the late mail drop before midnight, with both of us still writing the certified labels in the back of the cab." She pointed to a sign on the wall that said LACK OF PLANNING ON **YOUR** PART DOES NOT NECESSARILY MEAN AN EMERGENCY ON MY PART. "Tessa put it up. She liked the irony."

That made me like her. "I'm looking for her."

"How come?"

"I just want to make sure she's okay."

"She's fine," she said, "on vacation."

Ah, so Kristi was here alone, with nothing to do and no one to talk to but me. "Better than boredom" is a great position for a questioner to be in.

"On vacation? Really?" I said, as if I knew her better than Kristi did, and found that conclusion contrary to any hint I'd gotten in our long friendship. Tessa and I were, after all, closer in age. Recalling how hopefully she'd looked over when Mike blew the horn, I said, "New boyfriend?"

She hesitated.

I knew that kind of look. "Oh, God, not that same . . . what's his name?"

"Shit. She takes one vacation in three years and the asshole chooses the Friday before she leaves to break up with her."

"Wow."

"Yeah. I just get called to work here when there's overload and, yeah, we're dervishing around to get things done and afterwards we're too wiped to even go for a drink. But anybody who saw her staring at her cell phone, trying to call him that day, could figure out what was going on."

The cell that would have his number. The cell that, likely, was in her purse on the bottom of the bay.

"She must've tried him, like, ten times before he picked up. I don't know what the bastard said, but you ever see the air knocked out of anyone? I didn't believe that was real, but if you'd seen her it was, like, amazing."

"That's all she did?"

"She didn't get him till after noon, but, like, she'd try, get voicemail, look at the computer, then tell me to go get postal supplies, the kind we get delivered any other time. Then she'd call, check the computer, look at the phone like she was going to try again and then stop. She sent me out for sandwiches, told me to take my time, look around, like she wanted to talk to him alone, if she got him. But when I came back I heard her."

"Heard what?"

"She was begging him to reconsider. 'Isn't there another way?' 'I know I promised, but there's got to be another way.' It wasn't like she had much hope, you could tell, but she had to try." She took a sip of her appalling tea.

"You know, like, I'm like half her age and I can tell the guy's a real loser. But, like, girls don't want to hear that until, like they want to hear it, you know?"

I looked at her with new respect.

"Still, you must've felt awful for her."

"I really did. She looked so drained. But what could I do? I mean, I'm just her assistant here. I just wished I was still out getting lunch. She said something like 'yeah, okay, okay.' At the end, though, she had one little burst of life. She actually smiled when she said, 'I will enjoy it. I'll be the first lady of enjoyment. And yeah, it's still worth it. So don't worry about me.'"

"Strange. So, what'd she do when she got off the phone?"

"Turned on the computer again. It was like she forgot I was there." She sipped her tea, and in the gloom that encompassed us I would have been glad of something warming to comfort me, even that stuff.

But the gloom was a bond of sorts. I said, "Kristi, let me ask you, what's your take on Tessa?"

She looked startled. "She's better'n this place, that's for sure. Better'n twenty bucks an hour. And dealing with the lawyers who're freaking out, that's like . . . she's great. Takes no crap. Sometimes she even spots mistakes. I mean, she's smart. She could've gone to law school, or something, anything better than this."

I nodded knowingly, as if this was a familiar trait in the woman I'd known for years. "What's she doing now with the rest of her time? What's she into these days?"

"She did that collage. She's got a good eye, but, well, paper's cheap. I mean she doesn't make a fortune. But, it's not like she's stingy, I don't mean that. Like, she always buys a *Street Spirit*, every day."

To give the homeless seller the buck.

"Like, we had a mad rush a couple of months ago, huge, a mess, full of mistakes, motorcycle couriers back to the lawyer's office three times. We

66

ran out of paper and, well, even she was crazed. At the end the lawyer gave her a big bonus, two hundred bucks. Know what she did? She insisted on one for me, fought for it. Got me a hundred bucks."

I nodded. But that red jacket of hers couldn't have been cheap even in a secondhand store. And it sure hadn't looked worn.

Kristi was off on another tack. She lowered her voice, though there was no one around but us—"Besides, no one's going to hassle her on this job."

"How come?"

"A few weeks ago this client comes by to pick up his order. It's a big one, a rush, some two-sided copying, some color. The thing was a bitch, and since it was a super rush job the bill was plenty. He squawks, squawks loud—highway robbery, he's not going to pay, does she think he's a fool? The whole deal. He grabs his copies and charges out, just as Tessa's boss, the guy who actually owns this business, is coming in with our checks. He's heard the whole thing. He takes the squawker aside, talks to him, hand on his shoulder, never raises his voice. But in five minutes asshole's back, payment in hand. Like an illustration for 'tail between his legs.'"

"What do you think went down?"

"Dunno. But the owner, he's not someone to fool with, and Tessa—she's got a pretty good relationship with him. I mean she runs everything here. All he does is bring the checks by. But once she said he's not someone you want to cross."

"Who is he, the boss?"

She stared into the cup in front of her as if she was about to read the leaves. From her wary look, they weren't going to bring good news.

"Kristi?"

"Uh uh. I said too much. I'm not going there."

You're afraid to mention his name? Or was she just caught up in the drama? I really wanted to know. For now, though, I needed to dial back.

"So, besides the guy who prefers not to answer his cell, what does Tessa care about now?"

"Got me."

"What'd you talk about, I mean, besides work?"

"Me." And then she laughed. "Jeez, I never realized that, before. Me! I didn't realize . . ."

"Lots of people never realize. You're more perceptive than most."

She eyed me with a mixture of suspicion and pride, as if I was trying to flatter her, which, of course I was.

I'd learned more about Tessa, but I was no closer to finding her. I had to take a chance. I said, "Did you know she gave away all her clothes?"

"All her clothes?" She repeated the words like she couldn't fathom their meaning. I didn't blame her. She didn't know what I did about Tessa on the bridge.

"She doesn't have family out here, does she?" I, her supposed friend, should have known that, but I had to ask.

Kristi hesitated only an instant before saying, "No. None . . ."

"None. I do know that. She had some decent job back east; then she got lured out here by some fat Silicon Valley offer and then they laid her off."

"When?"

"Years ago." She bit her lip.

"But?"

"But what?"

"There's something more to this, isn't there? Something that makes it worse, something she said . . . ?" I was all but holding my breath, trying to draw her in, to not break the mood.

"I don't know."

"Family? You were saying she had no family? Maybe she left them back east?"

"No. Not . . . I don't know."

"I think you do."

"Wait a minute! Who are you to—"

"Kristi, she tried to kill herself last night. On the bridge."

"You mean like . . . jump?"

"Exactly. I pulled her back. That's how I know her. That's all I know about her. Except that I've got to find her before she tries again."

She was trying to mesh this news with the Tessa she knew. I could see her succeeding. She shrank back away from me. "You lied to me. You just wanted to make me talk. What's going on? How do I know you're telling the truth now?"

"I'm sorry! I'm the one who pulled her back! Kristi, she could be heading back to the bridge right now! Help me! Help *her!*"

She hugged her cup to her chest and for a moment I thought she was going to cry or scream. "Omigod, she really tried to kill herself? I know things were bad with her boyfriend but—Omigod! The bridge!"

"This is important! You thought she seemed fine for a while. Did you mean that or were you just trying to blow me off?"

"She did. Let me think." She was pretty rattled. "One thing made her, like, insanely happy last week. Just last week."

"What?"

"A Campagnolo Mirage."

"She got a racing bike?" Boy, was that not the answer I'd been expecting. And yet, there'd been a bike on the bridge that was gone after she disappeared. And she'd sure disappeared fast. "You saw it?"

"'Course. You don't leave a bike like that outside, even chained. It was a bitch, though, the way it took up space against the wall over there. Us trying to stack copies, move them, check them, not crash into it. Any other time, like, she'd've been going crazy with something impeding a rush order, but last week she just laughed. She actually said—I would've bet real money these words would never come from her mouth—'If it's late, it's late. They'll live.' Then she grabbed the bike for a half an hour ride, in the middle of a rush job!"

"But why all of a sudden the bike?"

"Didn't say."

"But you *think* . . .?"

"I figured it had something to do with college. She'd go on the college website, Dickinson College in some little town in Pennsylvania, and I dunno, it was like somehow the bike connected to it. Like maybe she was getting the bike to go back to school. But, you know, that's wrong. She was caught up in the college thing, intense about it. But with the bike, she was just happy. It'd make more sense to say she was going to college in order to ride her bike."

"That's so weird. It makes no sense. And it won't until I find her."

"Well, I'm not her keeper. I like Tessa, but I don't see her outside work. I sure don't follow her home."

"There's got to be something around here with her address on it? Like her pay stub."

"Yeah, but she didn't leave her checks here. She stuck them in her purse like any sane person."

"There's got to be something," I said, desperately. You don't work with a woman and not at least wonder where she lives. That's just normal. "Oh wait, the owner, he'll know," I said triumphantly. "How can I find him?"

"Are you sure—"

"Kristi, she tried to kill herself!"

She hesitated before pulling out a card and handing it to me.

When I saw it I understood.

12

HER STOMACH'S CLAWING at her innards; it's the feeling she had before when things went bad, when all that mattered was riding fast. Before, she'd either been starved or stuffed—in food, in life. Back then mornings had started with hangovers and Turkish coffee and ended with who-remembered? The first few miles were always hell till she'd burned through the bad. Then it'd been like sailing.

She waits now for the end-of-the-hour feel-good story to air. She's in the repair shop, inches from the TV, leaning forward to punch up the sound. She still can't believe she'll get to see it. The ceremony was at 10:00 AM. She'd been invited. She'd never have gone anyway, even if she hadn't had the world's best reason: *Tessa Jurovik regrets she must decline your kind invitation because she will be dead.* Now, seeing it on TV will be perfect.

She is about to see Ginger Rampono walk across the stage.

The station is coming out of commercial, back to the news set. Three minutes before the hour. Now!

But there's no stage, no Ginger, nothing. Just a recap of the headline stories. Didn't they get the film in time? They had an hour and a half, plenty of time even if they had to drive it back to Oakland through traffic. Maybe—

She pulls out the phone that isn't hers, turns it on. There's another message. She ignores it, gets the station number, hits it in. When the receptionist answers she realizes she doesn't know who to ask for or how to make them talk to her. "You didn't run the Ginger Rampono story," she blurts out. She knows she sounds frantic, crazy. She throws herself back into who she was last week, telling a man no, she wouldn't drop everything for his order, that he could take his business elsewhere. "It was scheduled to run just before the break during the last segment. I need to know why it didn't and when it's been rescheduled to. I need to know *now*." The authority in her tone is absolute.

"Do you have an update?" the receptionist asks her.

Update? That makes no sense, but she's not about to say no. "Right. Who's doing the story? Is it"—frantically she tries to recall the reporters' names—"the dark-haired woman, the pretty one?"

"Andrea? No."

"Let me speak to the station manager."

"I'll see if she's—"

The phone clicks and for an instant she worries she's been cut off. Then a voice, echoing her own authority, says briskly, "You have an update on the Rampono story?"

"Tell me what you've got so far."

"Nothing. Canceled."

"Canceled? Why?"

"The young girl, Ginger, was in an accident this morning."

She goes stiff. She can barely get out words. "Accident? What? Is she okay?"

"I thought you'd be telling us that. Your update—"

"What kind of accident?"

"A car clipped her in a crosswalk—"

"Was she injured?"

"Of course. When you get knocked down, of course there's some injury. Look, either you know something about this or not, and if— "

She does, she knows a lot. She clicks off and stands staring at the phone, as if it's going to tell her more.

It is. She sees the message again and this time checks it. She recognizes the number and the voice that says, "Tonight. Do it."

Tonight.

She knows all too well who the hit-and-run driver was. And she's clear that her freedom today is an illusion. Five hours from now, she'll be on the bridge. There's no escaping.

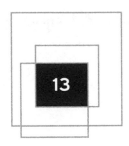

13

THE HALL OF Justice was less than a mile away. I stopped outside and looked again at the card Kristi'd given me. My stomach clutched.

The guy at the desk was a friend of my oldest brother, John. They'd been rookies together. Then Sam'd been a freckled kid with straight sandy hair he'd failed at greasing back. Even to me, barely a teenager, he'd looked not yet formed. Now he looked like he'd melted—hair gone, skin sagged, even those freckles faded. Despite infuriating an array of cops and city officials over the years, John had made detective ages ago. What had happened to Sam that he was riding the desk?

When he smiled up at me there was a flicker of those days of hope and energy. "Hey, there, Darcy, how's the movie business?"

"I set up a car gag this morning. Had a street sign in fear of its life. How're things with you?"

"Good as they can be. Haven't seen your brother in a while, though." He didn't add, "Not since John got all that publicity a while back, since he became a big hero."

"He'll be glad I ran into you." I couldn't help but linger a moment, remembering the days when coming to the Hall of Justice to see my big brother at work had been exciting and John and his buddies had formed a blue wall of safety around me. But that was decades ago. Now I took a deep breath and said, "I need to see Declan Serrano."

Suddenly Sam wasn't listening. He was staring as if a giant crater was opening in my forehead.

"Sam?"

"Does John know about this?"

I shook my head.

He shot a glance down the hall. "You sure you want to get involved with him?"

"It's just a quick question. No biggie."

When he didn't move, I said, "But I need it now. Is he here?"

"I'll check." He lifted the phone, still eyeing me like something alien. "He's in. Down the hall, last door on the left." Before I could thank him, he pushed up and walked over to a clerk and started talking. If I was making a bad choice he wasn't going to be in line for the backlash.

I hurried down the hall. Every sensation seemed heightened. Cops' leather shoes didn't merely hit but drummed against the floor, ringing cell phones echoed off the walls, guys barked orders like machine guns firing. Even the smallest woman looked huge in her stiff blue uniform, overlarge belt with holders and holsters protruding like pontoons. The last time I'd been down this hall it'd been to view the meager effects of a woman I'd thought would be a friend, not a corpse. I didn't look at the door to the viewing room as I passed, or at the people on the benches. When you're waiting in the Hall of Justice, the best you can hope for is to walk out alone, angry or bereft. From there the options go downhill.

I stood in front of the door. DECLAN SERRANO, it proclaimed. I'd never met him, even seen him, but I'd heard the name often enough from John, and Gary when he'd been acting as John's attorney in a corruption mess. Declan Serrano had been up to his nostrils but he'd managed to keep breathing and doing it in a corner office. He was, John had insisted, too well connected to ever get his head pushed under. He'd outlast everyone. The cockroach of corruption, someone had called him. Now, in our house, he was just known as the cockroach.

"Can I help you? You're Lott's sister, aren't you? The stuntwoman?"

It took me a moment to recalibrate my mental image of the cockroach to the guy popping out of his chair with hand extended to me. His head was shaved, his nose so straight and wide that it seemed like a long tube cut off above his mouth. He looked like a frat boy headed to the basketball court.

"I'm here to see Declan Serrano."

"Got me! Come on in. Let me get this file out of the way." The folder was bulky and frayed at the corners but he slipped it into a drawer as easily as if it were an envelope. The office was standard issue, but spotless. If I hadn't seen the folder I'd've wondered if he worked in here at all. There were no pictures, no placards, nothing but the sign on the door to say this was his. He motioned to a substantial metal armchair. "Sit, sit."

I know better than to sit in the seat of the enemy, even one as enthusiastically welcoming as he, *especially* one as surprisingly welcoming. I propped my butt on the chair arm. "So you underwrite Skilled Copy on Cunningham."

"How'd you connect me?" He'd had a smile in place but for an instant it slipped. Now that cute, flat, frat boy nose looked reptilian and the eager brown eyes had narrowed momentarily, removing any hint of innocence. I could see him, as an enforcer, playing both sides, cutting deals, cutting out colleagues and stabbing them in the back. I blinked, and he was the eager friendly guy again.

No way was I dragging Kristi's name into this. I used an exercise from an acting class a few years ago—Mimicking the Speaker. Then we'd been able to stare, but now—not. I glanced at his face, and flashed the feel of it on my own. Maybe seeing my unguarded thoughts pop up in meditation had shown me I was as much a phony as anyone else, or maybe I was truly reflecting him. "I've done a bit of detective work."

"Stunts and sleuthing."

I flashed a false grin. "I could sleuth into whether you own the property or if it's leased to the department. Or something else. But that hardly seems worth my time, since I have a hard time believing you're just encouraging small business. So what is it?"

Before he could open his mouth I realized the answer. "A front."

I was ready for hard-hitting denial, but he shrugged. "Yeah, a front for . . . for us." He settled in his chair and again motioned me to slide down into mine, as if he hadn't just asked me to sit a minute ago. "A very good front. With legitimacy we couldn't buy."

"Lucky."

"Lucky."

"Or not just luck?"

"Yes and no. Luck that I spotted her, luck she found a guy to underwrite her business. Luck, well no, not just luck that she handles that business well. Competence."

"On both your parts?" *I spotted her*—odd choice of terms. I could ponder that later. This sparring was a quick in-and-out game. "I need to find her."

"Why?"

"She tried to jump off the bridge."

"The Golden Gate?"

"I happened to be there. I pulled her back. I think it's her."

"You *think?*"

"She didn't leave any identifying . . . anything. There're probably pictures on the bridge cams."

"What's it to you?"

The sparring was over. Now it was for real. I waited a moment, then told him what he'd know that I knew he knew and what it explained. "When someone goes missing you think there's a point that you'll adjust and go on with your life. There isn't. We waited for Mike every day. There was never a time we didn't wonder what we did wrong, what we missed, what we said or didn't say. Trust me on this."

He hesitated and in that moment I knew he'd been planning to stonewall me. He was taking advantage of the pause to decide how to play it now.

I didn't have time for that. "Tessa said she'd try again! It's already afternoon. In a few hours she could be back there climbing over the rail. *Your* employee, the woman you say you spotted."

A hint of a smile flickered. "You think I'm callous?"

"I don't think about you at all. Look, I'm just asking for her address! I don't really even know if it's her. Maybe I'll go to her house and she'll be in her bathrobe drinking coffee, reading the *Chron*."

He didn't reply. I could see him still trying to figure out the damage control.

What're you more concerned about than her life? Is it your precious front? Or maybe—"Tessa, is she a cop?"

"Hell, no!"

"Cops aren't suicides? Give me a break."

"Cops off themselves, Darcy. But they don't have to jump from bridges to do it, not with a forty-five in the holster, a private in the glove box, and narco down the hall."

"So you have civilians working in your fronts?"

"That's what fronts are."

"You're telling me you hire people off the street? So you could be hiring me?"

"Not after this."

I laughed. "Tessa's address?"

Unwarned, I'd have taken him as a pleasant lightweight. But he was better than just a good cop who'd mastered the poker face. He was maintaining character and running his thoughts behind it, a front operation of his own. "Okay, but you're going to owe me."

If I hadn't known better—

I did know better. Favors in the cop shop are a whole different animal than favors in wine bars. Declan Serrano was one guy I definitely did not want to owe.

And yet . . .

He pulled open a file cabinet and poked around. "I'm doing this as a favor."

"I could Google her. But thanks."

"A favor."

"Thanks. If you ever want a pass onto the set when we're doing a stunt, let me know. If your kids—"

"A pass, yeah. I'll let you know. Or I'll let your brother know."

I shook my head as if amused. "We're big people, Declan. You can deal directly with me."

"Really?"

"Yeah. The address?"

He masked up with that smile again. Did it always hide the same thing? With luck I wouldn't find out.

I took the paper, gave him my best fake expression, and walked out.

The question was, what was he going to do now? He'd already gotten on the horn. Outside, eyes would be on me and they'd stay on me at least till I cleared out of Tessa Jurovik's apartment.

Why not make it easy on myself?

I retraced my steps back inside, past Sam at the desk, who looked up then quickly away, and on to Serrano's office. "You've already got a guy on the way there, right? Cut out the middle man and give me a ride."

He looked up and grinned, this time for real. "There's a burrito truck outside just south of the main door. Pick me up a carnitos with extra hot and you're on."

14

ONLY AN IDIOT gets into a police car unless he's driving—another of my brother John's dicta. Hey, in for a lamb, in for a sheep.

Or was it *hanged* for a sheep instead of just a lamb?

Whichever, when I got to the front of the line at the Carnitos Burritos truck, I opted for the chicken burrito, and got the special for Serrano, adding a couple of Cokes, Mexican Cokes—from the old recipe with sugar not sucrose, that gives more bang for the buck.

It'd been many hours since my donut on the set. Had the day been decent the sun would have been midheavens. It doubtless was, lounging atop the fog. Like so many San Francisco days this one had started out overcast with the promise of clearing—i.e., it had lied. If I hadn't had so much food in my hands I would have pulled my jacket tighter around me.

When a black unmarked car, the kind that marked the driver as SFPD, pulled up I was glad to slide in and pass him his share of lunch.

He eyed my half-eaten burrito. "You got time." But before I could take a bite, he said, "What's with that guy Dale?"

Uh oh. "I don't know. Blowing the horn like that—"

"Horn's the least of it. Asshole called City Hall. Wants to file a complaint!"

"What?" I didn't know where to begin being outraged. "Sorry. He's got no business—really, sorry."

"Tied up half my morning."

"Sorry," I said and took a conversation-blocking bite of burrito.

As we drove down Mission Street, there were plenty of distractions. Best time for questions. I started out slow. "Where'd you spot Tessa?"

He corralled a bean with his tongue. "More like I was crushed into her. At last year's Lit Crawl—one of the readings at Muddy Waters. So mobbed the author was yelling and you still couldn't hear her."

"Pulling overtime?"

"Cops can read, or maybe you didn't know that."

Touché. Declan Serrano might be an aficionado of the city's literary scene but nothing I'd ever heard about the cockroach suggested that. Still, I felt like an oaf. I took a swallow of Coke and did a mental reset. "So you ran into Tessa, and what? Asked her out?" Could he be the boyfriend?

"Nothing that formal. Just coffee and business. Enough for me to know she was right for what I needed."

"How so?"

He took a big bite, but a slower bite. Not a good sign.

He'd been answering so automatically, why was he hesitating now? "What do you know about her?" I prodded.

"She's just one of my employees."

Oh, please! "An SFPD officer doesn't run a background on the woman fronting his operation?"

"I can read people. It's my business. If I couldn't I'd be dead thirty times over. Took me one look to know she was right."

"Really? What'd that look tell you?"

He lifted the burrito and took a bite that would keep him busy chewing for blocks.

84

It didn't surprise me that he wasn't answering—what stunned me was his evasiveness. I'd've put money on his first reply being, "Fuck off." By the time he swallowed and said the meaningless "She looked competent," I was barely listening.

What had he *not* said? "Where'd she come from? Surely you ran a social security check, asked for employer references."

Another big bite.

I didn't have time to wait out his lunch. The guy could nod or grunt. "Back east?" Could she be from Pennsylvania? Near Dickinson College? Was that the—

"Toledo."

"Ohio?"

"What'd you think? Spain? Yeah, Ohio."

"What'd she do back there?"

"Minor offense."

I almost choked. I'd meant her work, not her rap sheet. I swallowed fast, too fast, and had to grab for my Coke while he looked at me and laughed. "What kind of crime?"

"That's more than you need."

"What? Her committing a crime makes her a good employment prospect?"

"For me, yeah. You got a record, you don't want to mess with the cops." At that moment, he screeched to a red light, turned, and gave me such an innocent smile it sent chills down my spine.

As he hung a left off Mission onto a side street, I asked, "How'd she seem to you recently? Depressed, desperate, hopeless?"

"Normal."

"Which means?"

"Means that I only saw her when I went by there."

"How often? Daily?"

"Whenever." His phone buzzed. His phone rang. He ignored it. "Leave a message," his message said.

Almost immediately it buzzed again. He picked up. "What?"

I couldn't hear the caller, which was fine. Time was running out on this ride and I needed to think. When he hung up, without a word, I said, "Why would you even go over there? If she's not a cop, if she's just staffing the front, you have no reason—"

"Don't be telling me what I can't do." Suddenly, he shot the car to the curb, slammed on the brake. "Let me make something clear to you. Don't think this is a free ride just 'cause you're sitting there. You don't like it, get out."

"And yet, Declan, your employee just about kills herself. You don't know why. You don't know where she is now. What does that say about you?"

"Watch what you—"

"She was supposed to be going on vacation. Where?"

"I don't—"

"You don't *know!* She's answerable to you, there on her own, in your front. Under your protection. What kind of big shot are you?"

He slapped me.

I was so stunned—

He stared as if to say: What're you going to do about it?

"Or," I said, "are you the boyfriend she was calling the Friday before she tried to jump?"

He grabbed my arm. "How do you know about that?"

"Are you?"

"Tell me!"

"She told me, on the bridge. What do you think?" I thought that might shake loose the truth. I didn't think he'd hit me again.

"Told you what? What'd she say?"

I was in too deep. Too deep to lie anymore. "That's all. You can waterboard me now."

It was an effort for him to rein himself in. He said, "If you think you're protected because of John, think again. I know your brother, known him for years. Knew him when he was a high school kid running smack down here."

"John wouldn't—"

"Not John."

I couldn't help myself, I gasped. *Smack.*

He'd gotten me. "Yeah, Mike. Said he needed the money." He laughed. "That's what they all say, as if that makes everything okay."

"He didn't need money. He always had . . . " *Shit!*

"He said"—he paused—"he did it for you."

I worked to steady my breathing. It was a moment before I could force out, "Yeah, right. If you'd had something on my family you'd've used it ten times over by now." I reached for the door and was out before he could react.

But he'd gotten me big time. I knew it. He knew it. The statute had run out long ago on anything Mike had done back then, but still it sent another chill down my spine a lot colder than fear of Declan Serrano.

I didn't even waste time not believing him. When I'd been desperate for private gymnastic lessons Mike had paid and we'd told Mom they were free. When I'd've died if I couldn't see the Up Down and Over auto race outside L.A. he'd arranged it. And there were birthday dinners for Janice, one at the Palace Hotel for Mom. Not often, but not cheap, and always with an excuse the recipient believed. And that was all twenty-five years ago. What had he been into since?

I wanted to figure—

But no time now. Now I wanted to get to Tessa Jurovik's apartment before Declan Serrano pulled up.

No way was that going to happen. Not with him in a car and me on foot. And, more pressing, I had to get to Kristi. I'd been so careful not to bring her into it, but a detective'd have to be a total dud not to make the connection.

I pulled out my phone, called information for Skilled Copy, let the phone company steal a buck for putting me right through.

It rang and rang, clicking off just before the machine picked up.

I'd thought to ask her for her cell, though. I called and left a message. And told myself that there were ordinary enough reasons she wasn't answering.

15

WHAT I COULDN'T stop thinking about was Declan Serrano's slap. If he'd take the chance of hitting me, his colleague's sister, what would he do to someone like Kristi?

Or Tessa?

I tried Skilled Copy again, not expecting an answer now, and not getting one. Ditto her cell. I could barely keep myself from racing back over to make sure Declan Serrano hadn't gotten to her.

But I wasn't near there or close to any transit that'd get me there. On the other hand, Tessa Jurovik's address was three blocks away.

I started to run, then caught myself. Whatever Tessa was into with Serrano wasn't going to be changed by my questions to him. I didn't want to burst into her place on his heels. My aim was to slither in after.

What would I do then? What did I expect? Who the hell was Tessa Jurovik anyway? I had three blocks to come up with answers.

Last Sunday Tessa Jurovik—

No, start earlier. On the Friday before that she'd had a fight with her boyfriend. With Declan Serrano?

No, before that. The weekend before last—Tessa Jurovik had bought a six-thousand-dollar bicycle. When she rode it she was *alive*. She rode it till the last possible moment, before she tried to jump off the bridge. The bridge is at the far corner of the city from the Mission district, but hardly an impossible ride. San Francisco's only forty-nine square miles. The hypotenuse of a right angle triangle is the square root of the sum of the squares of the other sides, right? So then, nine? Ten miles? Anyone on an old Schwinn could handle that.

And . . . ? Tessa Jurovik knew bicycles. You don't wander into a store cold and buy a top-of-the-line racing bike, one that looks no different to the untrained eye. So, this woman who spent her days copying paper knew bikes.

I started across the street. A car shot around the corner, just about blowing me back onto the sidewalk.

Just a car, not Serrano.

So, she bought the bike, but why now? A couple of hundred dollars' bonus wasn't the reason. Why buy a luxury bike right before a vacation? I couldn't get the pieces I had to fit together. What bothered me almost as much as Tessa's decision to kill herself was trying to figure out the extent of Serrano's involvement.

The vacation? Had she planning to go with him? Could—I smiled at the thought—could it be that she pedaled off the bridge, caught a Bayporter to the airport, and was on the beach in Waikiki right now? And the hell to him? Could that be why Serrano had gone off the deep end? Maybe he didn't know she was gone?

This was her block. I scanned the street, but no sign of the unmarked. Still, he could hardly have come and gone so fast. Or could he? I eased closer to the buildings letting the shadows shield me.

Tessa's building was squeezed between a motorcycle repair shop and a slit-windowed brick rectangle that could have held just about anything. Its streetside windows had drawn shades. The entryway was on the side and the window next to it was not merely barred but bricked in. Not a place

I'd sit on the stoop after dark. Riding a Campagnolo here? That'd be not merely asking to be mugged, but begging.

The buzzers were labeled, GRAHAM–1, BYRON/JUROVIK–2, AND GONZALEZ/WASHINGTON–3. Was Serrano still around? It was a question I couldn't answer. I pressed 2. No response. Big surprise.

But then came a real surprise. I pressed the door handle and the door swung open.

The hall was gloomy. I could just make out the edges of that former window around an amateurish bricking in. A wail came from the first-floor apartment. The *first* floor. She lived on the second.

What kind of place *was* this?

The wail was louder. Whiny. Piercing.

Omigod. A bagpipe!

A bagpipe in the middle of the city! A bagpipe played by someone who shouldn't. A fucking bagpipe!

Now things fell into place: the separate building, the bricked window—the self-deception in soundproofing! As if! I wanted to think the ground-floor tenant—he *had* to be the owner—gave lessons to the tone-deaf who came through the unlocked door and thankfully went, as opposed to the source of those shrieks being himself. Well, no need to creep silently. I raced up the steps and pressed Tessa's bell. Could it even be heard? How could anyone live here? Did Serrano pay her that little? Poor Tessa. What kind of life did she have? Her days spent copying papers and her nights in a place she couldn't hear herself scream.

"Yeah?" The guy who answered the door was young, with long dark hair and apparently wearing what he'd slept in. Headphones circled his crown, not earbuds but serious block-out-noise cuffs. He slid them to his neck. He was, of course, shouting. He'd either missed or ignored the downstairs buzzer—if it worked at all—but pulled himself together for the bell here.

"Tessa?" I asked.

"Out."

Had he given Serrano the same answer? "I'll wait," I mouthed and stepped forward. He moved reflexively and I was in the living room before he had time to reconsider. "This your—" the bagpipe suddenly went dead; I was shouting into silence but he barely seemed to notice. Behind him discarded clothes draped the sofa and cascaded over the floor. Tables held empty food cartons and quart-sized soda glasses. "This must be your room, right?"

"Not really. I mean, it's the shared space. Tessa, she could use it. But she's got her own stuff. I mean, I know it's a mess. My mom comes by with the rent and she tells me. Says I'm lucky to get anyone to share. Talks rats, health department, you know the spiel."

"When's Tessa coming back?"

He shrugged.

"Did she say anything about a vacation?"

"We don't cross much. I'm in school and—"

"Which school?"

"State."

"San Francisco State? You could hardly live farther away and still be in the city."

"Yeah, bummer."

A fresh bagpipe wail cut through me. I felt like my intestines were being yanked out. It stopped. But for how long? "How long?"

"Does he practice? Long as he wants. That's the deal. Rock bottom rent; never complain."

"How do you"—I shouted over the latest burst—"stand—"

"At school. Girlfriend. Hang out."

"Tessa, how does she?"

"Dunno." He fingered his headphones.

"Her boyfriend, does he come here?"

"No one comes here, not if they don't have to."

"No one comes to see her here?"

"Why would they?" He seemed anxious to block out noise, in this case me.

"She told me to wait in her room for her."

He jerked his head toward the hall.

The walls were covered with acoustic tiles, in the hall and—I pushed open her door—in her room. Which just meant that the noise came through the inadequate carpeting. I'd been expecting this room to be the size of the living room—Tessa's half of the apartment—but if it'd held a king-size bed, I'd have had to edge around it. It didn't. No bed at all. There was a desk, a serious metal file cabinet, the kind that has folders left to right rather than back to front. Neat, tall stacks of papers on top, bigger, more irregular piles against another wall. And on the carpet, dirt streaks from two narrow tires. No landline. No computer, damn! I pulled open the closet and almost fell over a rolled mat. Her bed? How could she live here? Much less work here? Maybe she was deaf? No, of course not—she'd heard Mike's horn; she'd talked to Kristi and the woman at the resale shop. How could anyone with normal hearing endure this? Why?

The pipes screeched and kept at it. I could barely keep from running out, but made myself look through the closet. Of course it was empty, but for a pair of bike shorts. On the floor was a pile of blankets, sheets, pillow. I turned back to the room, hesitated, and picked up the pillow and shook it. Just a pillow. The sheets under it were just sheets. But under that—voilà!—was a laptop.

I shifted the nearest pile from the top of the file cabinet to make space. It was made up of college catalogs: Allegheny in Pennsylvania, Bucknell University, Lehigh, Lafayette, Muhlenberg, Susquehanna, all in

Pennsylvania. The next stack held schools in Virginia, and there were ones for Delaware, Maryland and New Jersey, and, finally, Ohio. What was this fascination with East Coast colleges?

A new screech made me slam my hand over my ears. Papers on the bulletin board shook. If there were an earthquake I wouldn't notice. If the building were attacked by terrorists I'd be dead before I realized it.

I moved the computer so I could see the door and turned it on. *Please don't use a password!* I prayed to the balance-in-the-universe gods, the ones who arrange for you to whip through town on all green lights—that after a day of all reds. And damned if they didn't come through—bagpipe payback?—not only to a screen but, after one click, right to Google. I had only to click on History to see a list of colleges that went on for pages. Websites showed one homey place for eager happy students after another. One after another students hurried or strolled though sun and snow, among pines and oaks. But never palms.

I checked the list more carefully. No state universities, no Ivy League schools, but, if the ones I recognized were examples, small liberal arts schools. Not one of them was in California.

Odd.

The noise stopped. The silence was piercing.

How long had I been here, in this stranger's room? I just hoped if she came back I'd hear her lugging her bike up the stairs. Quickly I skimmed down the history, now ignoring the colleges until I came to Bank of America. I clicked on the website, but of course a password was necessary.

I glanced nervously toward the hall. No one was there. I clicked on Documents, Self. *Everyone knows better, but please be one of the people who do it anyway!* And she was. There was a file titled *passwords*. Halfway down, under modem was "bank: Rmpn$ – g5ng5r." I'd owe the gods big time for this.

I was in! I could see her account history for the entire year. It told me nothing I couldn't have guessed. Slowly, and surely painfully, she'd made deposits of two to three hundred dollars swelling the balance till it reached $6,753.93. There'd been monthly checks of $200.00 to the Ginger Rampono Fund but no withdrawals until two weeks ago when she'd written a check to Central Cyclery for $6,532.99 and another, dated Monday, to Rampono Fund for $220.00.

The Ginger Rampono Fund?

I Googled. "Ginger Rampono was orphaned four years ago at the age of eleven. She was a passenger in the car when her mother was killed in one of the city's most dangerous intersections. Without relatives, Ginger has been placed in foster care. This fund has been set up to help with the kind of expenses foster care does not cover and to offer her a better future." The image accompanying it was a picture of a thin, brown-haired child in jeans and a sweatshirt. The look on her face said: You're making me do this, but you can't make me like it. She was all but sticking out her tongue.

It did make *me* like her.

I got out my phone and tapped in the number. The message recording was in a woman's voice, a soft voice, but breaking up. I moved to the window hoping the problem was dead spots in this building, hit redial, and waited, using the time to check the layout outside—garbage cans, fence, grimy stucco building beyond. "You've reached the office of Jessica Silverman, manager. I'm in the office Mondays, Wednesdays, and Fridays, from—"

The blow came out of nowhere.

16

I'VE HAD WORSE hits when stunts have gone bad. They say a knockout interferes with the circuitry so that the memory is never recorded in the brain. Maybe. But I remembered the crack on my skull, the sharp *thwack* and the muffled mess of noise, the green wave of incredible pain. I remembered lurching forward, grabbing for something to hold me up, and watching my hands slide down the window till I crumbled to the floor and hit my head again.

The blow had come out of nowhere—

Well, hardly. It had come from someone watching till I turned my back to the doorway, someone who knew where to stand and keep me in sight.

Now, seconds? Minutes later? The bagpipes still blasted. My head throbbed, and a mishmash of colors swirled. I felt the carpet underneath my hand, my head. I was on the floor! Automatically I jumped up and stood tall. *Injured? Not me! I'm ready for the next gag! Keep me on the payroll!*

The room was empty, the door open. I started to run down the hall. By the second step I was using all my concentration just to stay upright. Hands against the walls, I lunged forward. Blasts of bagpipe burst against my skull. I felt like I was in a war zone. "Hello!" I tried to focus, peering into the mire of the living room. Was he on the floor, out cold? Dead? "Hello!" I could barely remember what the guy looked like.

I steadied myself then lunged for the sofa and balancing against its side stepped around to the back, expecting to find a body crumbled behind. Nothing there! "Hey!" The noise stopped. I shouted into the silence. "You! Byron!"

"What?" he called from another room.

"Are you okay?"

"Yeah. Why?" He was in the doorway, holding what appeared to be a half-eaten peanut butter sandwich. He looked just fine, like nothing had happened. He stared at me. "Jesus, you're all bloody. Did you fall?"

"Yeah, I fell—after whoever you let in hit me!"

"I didn't let anyone—"

"I'm not making up this blood. So, either you answered the door and—"

"Door's open."

I turned. It was. "And you didn't find that alarming?"

He shrugged. "We leave it that way. Otherwise . . . I forgot to open it this morning. Almost didn't hear you ringing the bell. Before—a couple weeks ago—UPS tried three times and I never heard them. And that was about a computer I was waiting for."

I braced myself against the couch. Had I misjudged this guy? I had to make him believe I could still kick ass if I had to, but it was taking everything in me to do it. "Look, there are two of us, alone here, and someone hit me."

"Why would I—"

"Why would anyone?" The bagpipes let up. The sudden lack of noise buffetted my ears.

Why would anyone attack me? Who knew I was here?

Oh, shit!

I couldn't call the cops. I sure couldn't admit this to anyone in my family. In for a lamb, in for mutton stew.

Don't assume, Leo was always telling me. Odds were on Declan Serrano, but Tessa's roommate was right here. Still, why would he attack me? We were strangers; our only connection was her.

Maybe I wasn't the target at all. "Did anyone ever threaten Tessa?"

"Nah. Why would they?"

"People get threatened."

"Yeah, but like dealers or pimps or smugglers."

"There are stalkers."

He laughed, actually laughed. "Listen, no one's going to go after Tessa. Guys aren't fighting over her; they don't know she's there. She could be hot, but, trust me, she's not. Makes no effort."

I was having trouble listening. I'd started feeling queasy.

"She doesn't get out enough to piss anyone off. Like, her cell never rings. Living with her is the closest thing to living alone. Days go by without me even seeing her."

I let myself slump onto the couch proper and lean, thankfully, against the back. "Did she say anything about the guy she worked for?"

"We don't talk much."

"You live together."

He glanced at the room. "Not really. I mean we both have to live here, so we do. We're polite. But shoot the breeze? No. There are times I've passed her on the street and she hasn't bothered to say hello. Why should she? We're both in the kitchen here and we don't say hello."

I was watching for signs of unease or one of those odd tics liars have, but there was something else in his manner. "You don't talk *much.* Talk some, though, right? She said something a bit odd, right? Maybe a guy less perceptive would've missed it, but it made you what? Suspicious? Uneasy?"

"Don't fucking patronize me, like not keeping my eye on her means there's something wrong with me." He flung the rest of his sandwich toward a trash can, watched it wobble on the edge and fall to the floor.

"Come on!" I pressed harder. "There *was*."

"Okay, yeah. She called me."

"She had your cell number?"

"And I had hers. You know, like just in case. Like I could check to see if she'd be home when the UPS guy came. I mean, even with the door open they don't go sticking boxes inside. A couple times I ordered a pizza on the way home and needed her to pay for it."

"Convenient for you."

"That's what my girlfriend said. And yeah, it's true. But I paid her back and she didn't complain."

"But once she did call you."

"Yeah, and it was odd in itself. It's the only time."

"When was that?"

"Three days ago. She called. I didn't pick up. I was at my girlfriend's and I forgot the phone. So I didn't check messages until I got back here."

"What'd she say?"

"Nothing. I mean, nothing that mattered. 'Call me.' Something like that. But here's the odd thing. She didn't use her own phone. I didn't recognize the number and I knew hers because, you know, I'd called it a few times. Well, more than a few. But this was a different number."

"What'd she say when you called back? You did, didn't you?"

"Yeah, I did." He sighed. "I would've right away if I hadn't forgotten the phone. But I called as soon as I got the message."

"And?"

"She didn't answer. But here's the weird thing—the number she called from was at the Mark Hopkins."

"The Mark Hopkins Hotel?" *The Mark Hopkins Hotel on Nob Hill?* "She was having a drink there?"

"No. She was staying there. Room 1701. She spent the night there."

"She lives *here* and she spent the night at one of the priciest hotels in the city?" She'd emptied her bank account to buy the bike. How could she pay for a hotel room? "Had she ever stayed in a hotel before?"

"No way."

"Spent the night somewhere, just to get away from the noise?"

"If she could afford a night in a hotel she wouldn't have to live here."

"Point taken. So what'd she say when she came home?"

"She didn't. I mean come home. At least I haven't seen her. Not since then."

"Weren't you even curious?"

"You're thinking she was shaking up with some high roller?" He shook his head. "I don't know Tessa well, but I do know this: whatever she was doing there, there was a good reason, a good but tedious reason for it."

"But—"

"Believe me."

I pushed myself up and walked, still unsteadily, my head aching down the hall. Standing in her doorway, I kept trying to make sense of what happened here. Just before the attack I'd been looking at her bank account. Then I'd been looking out the window at the blank wall next door, trying to make out the Ginger Rampono Fund woman's message. But now . . . now, the computer was gone!

I walked back into the living room. "What do you know about Ginger Rampono?"

"Some kind of Thai food?"

"Tessa was interested in a girl with that name."

"Really?"

"Never mind."

I was halfway out the door, figuring which route I'd take to the Mark Hopkins, when I had a thought about what I should have asked first thing. "Where's her bike? Did she keep it in her room?"

"She had a bike? Damn, there are times I could've used that."

I'll bet, I thought. As a roommate you're as much use as a gerbil. And probably less curious. Did she live here in spite of that or because of it?

17

SHE'S ACROSS THE street, behind a Land Cruiser, leaning on the bike, keeping out of sight and watching the doorway to the building where she's spent so many ear-assaulting hours. Why was there an inverse relation between talent and volume?

For the first time since she got the word about the attack on Ginger, she thinks about the phone message. After she'd hung up on the Channel 4 person, she'd swung onto the bike and ridden. Just ridden. She hadn't intend to come here, she'd just ridden hard for downtown like she'd done before, leaning low over the bar, moving through the burn, choosing busy streets, weaving around buses, between cars, going too fast for thoughts to catch up. Five hours of life left; she hadn't wanted to waste it thinking *what ifs*. When she'd found herself in the Outer Mission, blocks from here, she'd thought of her old sweater. It wouldn't be as clean as that red jacket last night, but that wasn't her problem. It'd be freezing out there on the bridge.

But now she's thinking about the phone, the message from the airline, that tells her she was scheduled to fly to Miami Sunday morning. Maybe she's in the Bahamas, or Cuba, or the Caymans by now. Tessa Jurovik has flown off.

She clicks on the phone and puts in the number she recognized earlier. When it's picked up, she says, "Things are different now. Quite different.

You may think you've shown you can get to me any time you want, but I can get to you tonight. We need to talk."

She expects screaming, threats, but the whole conversation is business-like. As they both understand, the power has flipped. Now they're both on to the next move. "Where?"

She needs a place that's secluded, but not too secluded. She's not a fool. "Ferry Building, outside, by the north end wall. Five o'clock." She's terrified she's leaving too much time, time to do something to Ginger. Maybe she should—

"Can't then. Make it seven."

Seven—after sunset when the bridge walkway is closed. Too late to jump. She's going to be all right. She's going to be able to live! She can barely get the word out: "Okay."

She clicks off and leans back against the van. She's barely feeling anything now, not heat or cold, or hearing sound. She's exhausted, exhilarated, wary, very wary, and now that she's going to live, ravenous.

18

As I walked down the stairs to the sidewalk I could understand why Tessa's roommate, Byron, had leapt at the idea of an available bike—and why Tessa, doubtless, had never let him see hers. From the apartment it was a hike to the 24th Street BART station, farther to the J Church streetcar. There had to be buses but I didn't know them. If I'd thought there was the remotest chance of using Tessa's Campagnolo, I'd've made myself a pain in the butt over it, too.

A horn honked at the curb. "We're on!"

It took me a second to realize the man was calling to me, another to see it was Macomber Dale, the embodiment of self-satisfaction sitting in his Mercedes.

"On for what?"

"Get in."

I slid onto the lush leather seat and he pulled into traffic. "How'd you know where—"

"I'm ready when you are. How about now?"

My head throbbed; everything seemed surreal, most of all this sudden appearance of Macomber Dale.

"Called Elliot. 'sfine with him."

What was he talking about? All I wanted was to take a double dose of aspirin, aspirin with codeine or better yet morphine. It'd been a bad couple days for my skull. "You called Jed Elliot?" *Oh shit!* "About the stunt driving lesson? And he said—" I couldn't believe it.

"Call him."

"It's on your head," Jed Elliot declared when I got him on the line. "You were going to get specs on the Berkeley Marina. Where are they?"

Huh? I just caught myself before saying it aloud. I'd shoved that promise so totally out of my mind I had to fight to remember making it on the set this morning. Because . . . oh yeah: *You were going to get back to me with the contact info!*

Pointing that out would get me nowhere. "You're right. I screwed up."

Silence.

I still had a chance. "About the stunt driving lessons you've just okayed. Mac's not looking to improve his parallel parking. He's after celluloid time. When he does, he'll be part of the crew." *Your crew.* I laid out the words in as neutral a tone as humanly possible while sitting in the leather bucket seat of the subject, but I wasn't fooling anyone. Macomber chuckled. The negotiation, backing me into a corner, *buying* me, it was all part of the game. But my shock, that was a little lagniappe. He revved the engine and shot away from the curb.

"I trust you," Jed said. His words were as flat as mine. He wasn't taking the easy path of stretching my blame to include this. He was covering, but what? "We got the Marina."

"How did you manage that?"

"Macomber got us a deal."

Oh.

"It'll bring us in under budget. San Fran's going to think twice before they close me down again."

I'm screwed.

"It's a flat road. We'll clear the parked cars, get dummies. Worst can happen he hits a tree."

Worst that can happen? Words like that should never be spoken aloud. Silence buzzed on the line.

Mac cut left—too close—in front of an SUV. Too close, but not dangerously so, unless the driver was armed. A horn blared.

I tilted the phone so Jed could hear it. Mac grinned. Dammit, he knew he'd won.

But there were spoils to go around here. I grinned back at him and said into the phone, "And you're offering me . . . ?"

The phone clunked. Did he drop it?

"Jed?"

"Okay. Stunt Coordinator credit on the roll."

Stunt Coordinator . . . Darcy Lott. I could see it in the middle of the screen, right under Jed's name, before the crowded columns of stunt doubles and other fine-print entries. More to the point, directors would see it. It could be a big step for me, way more than merely scouting locations. I wanted to scream, "Yes!" But I said, "And pay?"

"Yeah, okay, stunt coordinator's scale. For the Berkeley shoot."

I turned to Mac to give him the update, but he was already so smug I knew he'd never questioned the outcome.

"Oh, and Darcy," Jed said, "Dale is inviting you to a charity thing for the movers and shakers in the city. Some of the up-and-comers'll be there. Can't hurt you to meet them."

"I'll do you proud." I clicked off and said to Mac, "This reception, formal or not?"

"Not."

"Okay. When?"

"Tonight." He shot through the intersection on the last instant of yellow. "So we can fit in a couple hours of driving before."

My head gave an extra hard throb. "Twenty minutes. You can drive me to the zendo."

"I'm not a chauffeur. I expect—"

Expect!

"Rule one: don't expect." Don't expect, i.e., don't assume! "So, I still need to know how you knew where to find me."

He grinned. "I have my ways."

"Which are?"

"No time for questions; you're only giving me twenty minutes."

"Answer and you get twenty-one."

He grinned smugly.

I don't give up; I postpone, briefly.

I pulled up every bit of energy and concentration I could muster through the pain waves in my head. "Alert? Good. That's what driving is, being alert. It's knowing your vehicle so well there's no you and no it. 'No horse, no rider,' they call it in Zen lore. You've got to feel it."

"Not a problem. This"—he tapped the dash—"is my baby."

"Fine. But the road, the parked cars, the weather, the traffic light, the kid who's about to run out between cars, the woman talking on her cell, starting across against the light: They've all got to be your baby."

"But that—"

"It's one baby, Mac. That's the secret." That was Zen, too. But maybe he needed a different metaphor. "All this, it's all your team. When Joe Montana took the snap he 'saw' the whole field. Didn't move his head, just was aware. That's how he knew where to throw the ball. All of this is your field: You ignore any part, and you're punting."

"Sure, but—"

"But even he had to learn, to practice. So, slow down; go with the traffic. Become *part* of the traffic. You already see the car in front; you're checking the rearview. Okay, what could come at you from the right?"

"Nothing, it's—"

"Parked car with driver up there. Guy with the dolly there, see? See? Now, across the street, what are you alert to?"

His forehead was scrunched with trying. His face was twitching. He wanted to succeed, to win. "No kids, no bikes, no one on cell phone—"

"You check for Blu-ray?"

"How can you possibly—"

"Posture, gait. See the guy in the green jacket? He's all ears—He's got tunnel vision because he's caught up in his call. If he could walk with his eyes closed he would."

"How can you drive and—"

"Practice. And silence. When you're stunt driving, you can't do anything else, not talk, not ponder, not even feel anything but the car. You had a punk meal and it's exploding in your gut—tough! Push it aside. You can drive or not drive. All or zip."

His shoulders rose, his face twitching like mad. He looked ready to let me have it. But he didn't. Didn't say anything. Just eyed the coffee house across the street.

I wanted to pounce. I postponed. "So, what's the combination of things that sends up a red flag?"

He continued to stare in the same direction.

"No! You've got to watch the road. You can't look out the window like a passenger."

"Don't do this! Don't do that! What the hell do you expect me—"

"Stop the car!"

He slammed his frustration into the pedal. Brakes screeched. If I hadn't been braced I'd've hit the windshield. Behind us more brakes squealed.

"How'd you find me?"

"I followed the cop car."

Across the street the bus swung toward the curb. A woman raced in front of us toward it, holding up a hand in Stop position.

"She didn't see you, didn't hear the horns. You're not even in her universe."

His hands tightened on the wheel. "*Fine*. I get it. But—"

"I wasn't in the cop's car."

"I could've picked you up when you slammed out of it, but you kept going in the same direction. I followed the car till it stopped—"

"Where?"

"Same place you did."

"Did he go in?"

"He followed a biker."

"A woman on a bike?"

"Yeah."

"Followed? Rode like she was leading him somewhere? Or tailed? Were they together?"

Mac shrugged. "She left, he left. You were my target."

"But you must've seen enough to get an idea."

"Why's it matter?"

I couldn't begin to tell him.

Horns blared. Mac jolted the car forward, nearly stalling out. He down-shifted, hit the gas, and shot daggers in my direction. "What's all this have to do with stunt driving? We'll have a blocked-off road in the Marina. No one's going to be running for a bus unless we pay them to."

I laughed. "This is Berkeley we're talking about. 'No entry' translates into 'Sez who?'"

"Yeah, but—"

"You're right about limited access. You don't have to watch two sidewalks and traffic in the slow lane, but you also won't be tooling along at twenty miles per hour on a smooth surface. No one pays ticket money to watch that. And those potholes. You think they're big now? We're going to be ramping up the sides. You'll have to angle into them, hit the edges hard. Then every minute you've ever driven is going to be commanding you to hold the wheel steady. Wrong! You've got to spin back—not *let it spin* but control it so it looks like it's gone haywire, so the chassis bounces the way *you* want it to. And do it one pothole after another, bang, bang, bang."

"But—"

"Meanwhile, hoping that passing pigeons, gulls, squirrels, and family dogs are obeying our signs."

He swung right following the curve of Mission Street into South of Market.

"Plus, you're not going to be driving your baby. Smooth handling? Think again. You know what they call the kind of car you'll be driving? 'More bounce to the ounce.'"

"Hey, I'm not here on a learner's permit."

"You are with me. Take it or leave it."

His face was tense, the cords bulging in his neck. I'd pushed him to the edge—I'd *enjoyed* it—but I'd left him no face to save. Chances were very, very good I'd pay later. *My* name was going to be on the credit roll. My screw-up gave him this chance. If he blew it, it was going to ricochet all over me.

"Turn left." We were at the Fifth Street mess under the freeway. It took all his concentration to cut through the line of cars hanging heavy lefts across traffic to the on-ramp, and do it before the light turned. There was a lot of no-man's-land here. But he was behind his own wheel and he was alert. "Focus in turmoil, that's what stunt driving is," I said for encouragement. Meanwhile, the intersection was buying me time while I figured where to get out.

The light changed. Cars poured off the freeway. On the cross street brakes squealed. I started, looked in time to see a bicyclist shoot through traffic with inches to spare as she cut left toward Market.

Dark hair, white T-shirt, black pants.

Tessa?

Or any of two thousand other women on bikes?

Just a T-shirt in November?

One thousand cyclists.

It was a .001 percent chance. But I had to take it.

"See that bike? Catch it!"

Mac looked at me. He eyed the cars in the lane to his right, the oncoming vehicles, the pedestrians on the sidewalk, and slowly eased the gas pedal down, gliding along with the traffic till it stopped dead twenty feet ahead.

I jumped out and ran.

19

"THIS PLACE IS like 'Call Me Central,'" I grumbled to Leo as I put down the landline phone. "My family . . . "

"Don't they know your cell?"

"They believe there's a better chance of getting a return on a call here. They believe you'll prod me to call."

Leo smiled, as if to say not yes, not no. He was sitting cross-legged on his futon, books lined up in front of him on a long rectangular *furoshiki,* one of the Japanese cloths used as bags, folded to cover gifts, boxes, and in this case books. Empty spaces in the bookcase revealed where the texts had been and now the *furoshiki* suggested they'd be wrapped and traveling elsewhere, though maybe only downstairs for lecture next Saturday. As his *jisha,* I'd be piling them in the center of the *furoshiki,* folding over both its ends and carrying them to a table next to his rectangular black *zabutan* in the zendo.

"My brothers believe," I admitted, "that I don't want to look irresponsible in front of you."

He swung himself around to face the wall in a surprisingly graceful manner, leaving me talking to his back.

I laughed. "But, Leo, I've got so much to do before I—"

"Before?"

"Right." I bowed to his back and stepped across the hall to my room. Time is an illusion; the future is a dream. And yet . . . I called my sister Gracie and reassured her about the rhubarb pie. It was already Monday night and I hadn't ordered one. There wasn't time now. First thing tomorrow I'd do it. Definitely, first thing.

I tried to get Jessica Silverman from the Ginger Rampono Fund, caught her only long enough to hear she was just rushing out the door and would be unavailable till tomorrow night, if then. "Busy week," she'd said with a sigh.

I called Jed to . . . It wasn't till I got his message that I realized what I really wanted to do was talk about how twitchy and volatile Macomber Dale was and what a bad mix he and I were right now. Just as well I didn't get through.

I got an earful from John about not returning his call, and then I played Gary's message and phoned to let him know his warning about John had come too late.

Only Mike hadn't been in contact, and after Declan Serrano's comments I was glad. I'd worry about Mike later.

Right now, my big coup was half an hour for a nap before the event with Dale tonight.

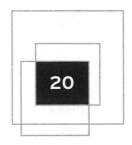

20

THE FIRST PERSON I spotted here amidst the movers and shakers was Declan Serrano, himself. Was there no cockroach-free zone in this city?

The reception was in City Hall rotunda, a spot best known nationally as the site of long lines of eager wedding parties during the brief periods when gay marriages were legal. Now, despite orange bunting and long tables of mild refreshment, the overwhelming sense was of chill, particularly for those of us flashily but inadequately dressed. Heels clicked on the marble floor and voices seemed to rise, swirl inside the dome, and bounce back down as a mélange of sound.

Mac handed me a glass of wine.

"Thanks."

"So, did you catch your cyclist?"

"Not hardly. If you can't beat a pedestrian, you shouldn't be on wheels."

"So, we could've had another hour practice time."

I nodded, not that it registered with him. He was busy doing the cocktail party scan. That suited me fine. In my heels I was just able to do my own over his shoulder, keeping Serrano in sight but at the same time maintaining my distance. He, though, was busy with a tall gray-haired woman in a silver suit, so intently focused he didn't seem to be scanning at all.

"Who're you looking for?" I asked Mac.

The clatter and chatter bouncing off the marble made it easy to miss anything said to me, or to pretend to. Without responding, he turned toward the dais and eyed the four guests of honor: a tall, striking blond man who looked too outgoing to be a nerd and, if not, then too young to have amassed enough of a fortune to give away; a frail woman in a dress the same green as mine; and the Saparitsas, who were parents of a woman who'd been in Mike's year in school. He'd once, long ago, been to a party at their house and when he stumbled back home at 2:30 AM he'd made such a racket he'd woken me up. Coming into my room, he'd leaned against the wall, sliding down till he was sitting on the floor, and started telling me about the place. The only thing I remembered now was that their house had more bathrooms than ours had rooms.

Mac was eyeing the lot like gaffers and techs do the lunch table (and actors wish they could).

"Checking out the field, Mac?"

I must've hit a nerve. He started, fussed over his wine glass, and said, "Women are better backers. Better prospects. Arty and all."

"Really?" I said with full bore sarcasm, but he was already off toward the dais on his own. There was an elderly woman up there but he wasn't looking at her. *Ah, so it's just hot babes who're the money pots.*

I'd've given him more thought if it hadn't struck me that a charity event like this was the type of thing Jessica Silverman might have been racing out to earlier. Philanthropists and those seeking generosity tend to frequent the same events. And how many would be scheduled on a Monday? I glanced around for someone who'd know her and ended up having a burst of conversation with the police chief, who drew a blank. I smiled at a deputy city attorney, then at the head of the Film Commission. But when I responded to a short, wiry guy he started a conversation that sent me onto the thin ice of white lies.

"You remember me, from high school? Warren Llekko? Doing great," he all but shouted. "Financial Counseling . . . Newsom"—the former mayor? Or not?—"downturn, no way. New projects . . . big money." One hand slipped around my waist, the other now waving to the blond man on the dais across the room.

"Aaron!" he called, for the benefit of those within five feet of us. "Adamé!" There was no chance of Aaron Adamé hearing. But Llekko's maneuver created a flurry in our spot, like a stone lobbed into a pool.

The honoree turned in time to trace the shouted summons to a man embracing a redhead half a head taller than he. A look of annoyance crossed his face. I wondered if Llekko noticed.

"Aaron's always making such a deal about how devoted a husband he is, how it's all for his wife. It's just his schtick. No one believes it, not about any guy like him."

Guess Warren did notice, after all.

"His wife's not even here. Guy gets a big honor and she blows it off. All for her, sure!" he added, with the righteousness of the recently snubbed.

Aaron Adamé's wife, who was also Macomber Dale's connection, i.e., the reason why Jed and I, and everyone else on our set, still had jobs. My ears perked up. "Why isn't she? Here, I mean?"

"One of those artsy, I-want-my-own-identity babes. Likes doing her own thing and then telling everyone else how to do theirs. Everyone's relieved when she doesn't show."

"Really? The wife of a big donor like that?"

"The luncheon."

"Huh?"

Warren did a broad double take. He was so clearly pleased with the story he'd get to tell that it kind of ruined his pose of insider disdain. "I thought *everyone'd* heard about it. Society charity luncheon, a dozen society babes, planning to aid hunger in the city. Outside, on the sidewalk, is a group of the unwashed hungry. Adamé's wife walks in just as the other guests are being seated, veers into the kitchen, has the waiters load the entrées onto carts, and wheels them out to the sidewalk."

I laughed.

"It was all over the media. She didn't even attempt an apology. Just arrogant. And clueless."

"That's so annoying, isn't it?" But, of course, he missed my point.

Enough of him! If Jessica Silverman was here and I missed her, because of Warren Llekko . . . ! I turned and asked a woman in a nearby group if she knew her. When she shook her head, I moved to another trio. But I didn't fare any better with them. Mac was visible on the dais haranguing the frail woman in green. Her back was to me, showing her stiffly hunched shoulders. Her whole posture said *long suffering*. Adamé was talking to someone though with nowhere near the animation. The two of them reminded me of the contrasting picture of girls and boys relating: the two little girls facing each other, the boys staring straight ahead but talking just the same. In all his gesturing and moving Mac had edged a bit in front of Adamé, and his whole being implored the frail woman: "Assure me I'm more than him."

Near the dais, watching, stood Declan Serrano.

I edged farther away, asked another group for Jessica Silverman, and a third. Despite my hunch I was startled when the next person I asked indicated a tall gray-haired woman in a silver silk suit with a sapphire brooch. It was the woman Serrano'd been with a few minutes ago. Close up she looked even more elegant. "Darcy Lott," I introduced myself. "I called this afternoon."

Jessica Silverman wore silver? It made me smile. But I could see why she'd made the choice. "As I said, I'm interested in the Ginger Rampono Fund."

If she thought I wasn't potential benefactor material, she was cool about it. There's too much new money in the Bay Area to be sure of anyone's status. "Ginger's fund's just that, a bank account set up for her. She's one of the girls under our overall umbrella."

I nodded. Few things are as easy as getting the head of any charity to talk about it. "You just got a large gift, I heard."

"A terrific one. Enough to send her to the perfect prep school and then on to college. If she's careful, there'll be enough for a year or two of graduate work."

As I made a properly appreciative face, she spotted someone, flickered her fingers in a wave, and looked slightly abashed as she turned back to me. "We do have reliable regular donors—our honoree's wife for one. He gets the attention—and well deserved—but she's created a small but ongoing payment fund for such young girls."

"For Ginger Rampono?"

"And others. But Ginger, yes. We were going to have a little ceremony this morning, right here actually, to honor the generosity of San Franciscans and show how one special contribution can change a girl's life."

The mélange of talk, silk rustling, and shoe leather against the marble floor was growing louder. I leaned in toward her. "All that for two hundred twenty dollars?"

"You're missing a couple zeroes and some change."

"Two hundred twenty thou? You sure?" I'd meant the two hundred and twenty dollars Tessa had sent, the twenty-buck increase from her monthly two hundred. What was she talking about?

"Believe me." She paused, lifted her glass to her lips, and considered me. She may possibly have drunk some of the wine, too.

"To be in that accident and then to be put into foster care . . ."

"So you know her?"

I made a sound too soft to hear over the buzzing echoes in the room, letting her translate it into what she wanted to hear.

She nodded. "Of course, virtually no child enters foster care without experiencing problems. But being with other kids acting out—well, I'm sure you get the picture. Ginger's the kind of youngster who might be overlooked. I oversee a lot of small funds for children, but with her, I worried. She needs someone to push her, to care."

"Two hundred thou! *Someone* cared."

"Yes."

"And Tessa Jurovik's two hundred a month—"

"How'd you know it was every month?" She was staring right at me, with a look of suspicion that seemed to surprise her every bit as much as it unnerved me.

How was definitely not a topic I wanted to get into. I went with the *know* part. "Tessa's contributions were all the more impressive considering how little she had herself."

Silverman hesitated. She still looked wary. Before I'd brought up Tessa, we'd been on safe turf, discussing nothing that hadn't been in the news at some point. Now discretion battled curiosity. I needed to push a bit.

"Do you know Tessa?" *As well as I do?* my tone indicated. I'd used this technique so often now I felt like I *did* know Tessa.

"Not really. Other than last Friday's call our contact's mostly been email. Once or twice she dropped off checks but I didn't see her."

"She must have been ecstatic when she heard about that huge donation."

Silverman hesitated.

"You told her, didn't you?"

"It's not our policy to reveal—"

"But surely, after all those years of penny pinching to make her contribution every month, *surely* you let her know."

"Please don't repeat this. But, as you say, how could I *not* share that wonderful news? Not the source. We never reveal a donor's name without permission. Not until the donor does, at any rate."

"Here? Tonight?" I couldn't believe my luck. From somewhere to our left I heard the sound of shattering glass. It was all I could do now not to turn, but I didn't dare break our contact.

Her attention shifted. "Weren't you with him?" She was looking toward the dais—looking at Mac.

He was on the dais, waving his arms, but to what purpose I couldn't tell. Nor did I want to know. I needed to get him out of here before he ruined not only his reputation but Jed's and mine.

Yet I was so close. "Jessica, will the announcement be here?"

"Here? No, no. This isn't that kind of event. It's small potatoes in this crowd, a couple hundred thou." As if to instruct, she informed me, "A contribution says as much about the contributor as the beneficiary. No one announces a gift without considering the economic, the social, and the business ramifications."

"But didn't you announce it this morning, at the little celebration you mentioned?"

For the first time she looked shaken. With great effort I stood silent and waited.

"Ginger"—she raised her voice over the roar behind me—"was nicked by a car in an intersection that morning and she was too upset—"

"Omigod, like when her mother died?"

"No, nothing like, except the intersection part. Ginger was just walking across the street and a bumper scraped her shin. She's okay. But she'll be glad to get out of the city. It was unnerving for her."

"So how's it *not* like the accident with her mother?" I'd raised my voice to be heard over the din.

"I thought you knew about Ginger. Don't you—"

"Just tell me!" I practically shouted.

But she was no longer paying attention to anything I was saying. Automatically I followed her gaze.

Mac was mimicking pulling up and back, and—oh shit!—pointing at me. He had to be carrying on about me pulling Tessa back on the bridge. I dropped my purse, bent down, and took my time getting back up.

Now Mac was shoving the honoree, Adamé. *Shoving him!* Like this was a schoolyard. There was a space around the two of them and the older woman honoree. She was too close to them. Adamé said something. Mac shouted. He grabbed Adamé by the shoulders and gave him a hard push, sending him backward. For an instant I thought Adamé was going to fall, but he steadied himself. He raised an arm. He was going to sock Mac!

I needed to get out of here fast. Do it before Mac's outburst engulfed me, our movie, and Jed's and my good names.

I grabbed Jessica Silverman's arm. "Ginger Rampono's accident today—how was it different from the one a few years ago?"

She looked startled.

"Look, it's a matter of public record!"

Still she didn't speak for a moment. "It didn't have to happen." She sighed. "Ginger was in the passenger seat. She wasn't wearing a seat belt. Her mother was driving. No seat belt, either. Mrs. Rampono swerved, hit the gas instead of the brake, lost control, slammed a wall. Just missed three pedestrians."

"Why?"

"A bike messenger cut in front of them."

"What happened to him?" *To her?*

I could guess the answer before she spoke. "Disappeared."

TIME TO KILL. Could there possibly be a worse concept? Time, every moment of it, is so magnificent. Time is spectacular—even if instants of it could be freezing. But she'd realized how to get clothes. And food. Now, full, and warm, she's standing at Coit Tower taking in the evening over the bay.

The bay that she is not moldering in.

She's on the bike, which isn't moving, and she's balancing. It's where she is right now, balancing between the open, free wonder of life and the tense focus she'll need for the meeting an hour from now. She's not afraid, though. She *would* have been a couple days ago, but now the power is hers. She won't be demanding much. She doesn't want money, she never did, not for herself, only for Ginger. She would have given her life for Ginger. And now Ginger will be okay. And she is still alive. Both!

But that crosswalk attack this morning had been a warning. One she needs to push back against hard. That's not going to be a problem. She has the phone and the power and she can expose everything at will. If she decides to, she can.

But she won't if she doesn't have to, she'll make that clear. She won't demand money. She's not passing judgment. It's just that after the last twenty-four hours everything's changed. She'll make her deal and pedal off.

She's not a fool. The meeting place has to be hidden from view, but she's chosen carefully. No one will be lurking in the shadows beside the Ferry Building, and yet there will be people within shouting distance. She can shout, attract passersby, shine light on what's happening; she can destroy the whole plan if she has to.

Or she can elicit the gift of a ticket, at which point she'll roll her bike onto the ferry, roll it off in Tiburon, and then pedal north into the rest of her life.

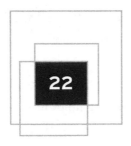

22

POLICE FLASHERS WERE lighting the damp pavement like early Christmas decorations. Brakes were squealing, squad car doors flying open. What had gone down inside was more squabble than serious. But we'd had the mayor and a supervisor shot in City Hall years before, and no one has forgotten. Any melee here is big stuff.

Out of one of the cop cars popped the last person I wanted to deal with: my brother John. If he spotted me, it'd mean an hour of questions, badgering, me hanging around, and him proclaiming he wasn't at liberty to divulge anything whatsoever to the likes of his kid sister. And when he discovered that the asshole who'd made a travesty of this high-powered charity event had arrived with me . . .

Not to mention the presence of Declan Serrano. Getting the chance to rag John about his sister's "date" in front of half the department would be more than a much, much better person than the cockroach could resist.

A cab skidded to a stop. A photographer jumped out. I leapt in.

"Where to?"

That issue hadn't entered my mind.

"You coming from this reception?" the cabbie was suddenly all eyes on the rearview, checking out my party duds.

"I'm going *to*," I announced. "To the Mark Hopkins."

If I had come back to the city after college, the venerable Mark Hopkins would probably have been just another venue to me. But after my twenty-year exile, stories from the far past unexpectedly cut into my thoughts. The one now, as the cab coughed up Nob Hill toward the hotel's floodlit entry, was of my grandmother dressing up to have a last drink at the Top of the Mark with her boyfriend, the two of them looking out the window and watching the sun set behind the Golden Gate before he shipped out to be killed somewhere in the Pacific in 1943. She had been much younger than I and yet I felt a—

But that was exactly what I did not intend to feel. I needed to head into the Mark Hopkins like I belonged there, like a woman who'd just come from a high-powered event in City Hall.

The cab jolted to a stop. I paid the driver and strode into the lobby, up to the great wooden reception desk. It was seven o'clock, well after the rush of check-ins.

Behind me, three couples were coming in, followed by a bellman pushing a luggage-laden cart. I strode to the counter, opting not for the newest-looking clerk, but the one more senior to him. The junior clerk was nabbed by a man behind me. "May I help you?" he said, with the politeness of the professionally courteous.

"My dear friend, Tessa Jurovik, was a guest the night before last. She thinks she left a notebook, a leather one with a design on the front. Would you see if it's been put aside for her?"

"I don't believe she's called, but let me check—"

"She couldn't. And now she's got a plane out of SFO in two hours. I said I'd do this for her." I looked at my watch.

"The concierge—"

"I understand. I'm sorry to rush in like this. But could you just check to see if anything was left in her room."

"I don't—"

"She just needs to know! If you can't give it to me I understand. Just tell me if she left it." I let my voice rise.

"I don't—"

Never let a clerk complete a negative sentence.

"Tessa had intended to stay at the Fairmont, but I told her she'd be much more comfortable here. The service, I said, is the best." Now I leaned forward and said in a stage whisper. "Don't prove me wrong."

Behind me, conversation stopped. It was a moment before the clerk said, "Certainly, madam, let me look into that for you."

He tapped three keys on his computer. "No record," he announced with clear satisfaction.

"J-u-r-o-v-i-k."

"I'm so sorry, madam, there's no record of anyone by that name."

"I dropped her off here Saturday. In this lobby. She telephoned me from her room. You have a record of her. Please find it." Surely Byron hadn't made this up. If he had, he was the one who should be doing the acting.

The man made a show of rechecking his computer. "I'm sorry, madam. I've looked at the entire week."

"It's an unusual name. Perhaps you've misspelled it. Try the 'G's'." No record of her, what did that mean? Odd enough she'd have come here, but now, to have *not* come? Could she have used another name? But that made even less sense. So . . . ? I was only buying time; the clerk wasn't going to find her under the G's or any other letter. And he was clearly anxious to move on to the increasingly less patient folk in line behind me.

But I couldn't leave here empty. What did I know about her? What would he remember?

"I'm sorry, madam—"

"Who was on duty here Sunday night?"

He hesitated. But I'd offered him an easy out here, particularly if the Sunday staff wasn't on duty now.

One of his younger colleagues spoke up. "I was on the desk then."

"Good," I said. "Then let me see how I can help you remember her. She's about my height, dark hair cut along the chin line, thin, about my age"—*What made her different, other than the bridge?*"—She's a biker—"

"Oh, the woman with the racing bike!" He gave a laugh indicating something peculiar.

"What?" I prodded.

"Well, uh, the thing is, we're at the top of a hill."

The couple behind me chuckled at this and, relaxing a bit, the second clerk said, "She insisted on keeping the bike in her room. Wouldn't even allow the bellman take it for her."

"So," I said, "you know she was here. Why don't you have a record of her?"

"Well, she wasn't using that name. She insisted on a room on our highest floor. That's not unusual, of course. But she wanted southern exposure."

I must have looked puzzled.

"See, most guests want views of the bay. But south, it's only the city buildings."

Not the bridge! "She didn't use that name?" I repeated.

"If you'd given me the correct name—"

"Which one?" I said, as if Tessa was an eccentric with a pack of aliases as well as a bicycle. "Saturday night in a south-facing room on the top floor." I couldn't give him time to think about what he was doing. "Was it . . . no, you go ahead."

He was staring at the computer but not responding. The man I'd been talking to originally was looking on.

"There!" The second clerk pointed to the screen. "Varine!"

"Ah," I said, "Varine?"

"Varine Adamé."

Varine Adamé? "Are you sure?"

"Certainly, madam, it's right there on her credit card data."

Varine Adamé? She skips her husband's ceremony and her card buys a night at the Mark. What did that say?

There was something about his expression that made me feel sure the guy had some inkling of memory about her, but I couldn't guess what. And his focus now was in moving me on. Behind me I heard grumbling. "Can I help you with some other matter, madam? If not . . . "

I shook my head. I walked across the lobby, stepped into the elevator, rode up to the nineteenth floor, the Top of the Mark, and ordered one of their hundred variations on the martini.

The tables by the windows were filled. So, I took one in the middle with a view of darkness, which was fine by me. If I'd been facing the wall it would have been even better. It was odd to be all dressed up here in the restaurant that had been such a romantic icon in city history, me, now, not staring into the misty eyes of a doomed lover, but desperate for a place to think.

I needed to think: a lot. I'd do it better with food. I went for clam chowder. Despite the ninety-nine idiosyncratic options, my martini was Grey Goose, vermouth with two olives. (There was a choice of a dozen varieties of olive. I went with green.)

I stared into the glass as Tessa herself might well have done and tried to imagine myself in her skin. But there were too many unanswered questions for me to make that leap. Who the hell was this woman who nearly jumped off the Golden Gate Bridge, who was a responsible employee at a bland job, saved her money, and spent it all on an expensive racing bike and a little girl she didn't know? And copped a woman's credit card for a night in the Mark Hopkins? The night before she was to jump.

I knew I should sip this martini. Instead, I took a good-sized swallow. I didn't expect it to clear my head but it did.

The one lead I had to Tessa was her hotel room here.

Maybe.

If the maid had missed something . . .

If no one had checked in later . . .

If, if, if. Not much of a lead, but it was all I had.

Or *might* have if I could only figure out how to get into the room.

A shadow moved over my table. I didn't look up, didn't even want to deal with the waiter. Too much time had passed since I'd pulled Tessa back from the edge, too long without her turning up anywhere. Maybe I would never find her, never know, the way it had been for so long with Mike. She could be deciding to go back to the bridge tomorrow.

I could not let that happen.

The shadow shifted. Irritably I glanced up, and gasped. Actually—embarrassingly—gasped. "What are you doing here?"

23

DECLAN SERRANO SLID into the chair across from me. In his suit and tie he looked only slightly out of place here—as if he'd mistake his knife for a shiv. But perhaps that was overkill.

The waiter arrived with my soup.

"That all you're eating? That's no dinner," he said, exactly as my brother John would have. Unnervingly so, in fact. He gave the menu the swift scan of someone used to being called to a crime scene before he could finish his meal. He made his choice—an exotic-sounding crab dish—without questions or alterations. He ordered it for two. For himself he added a martini with a vodka I'd never heard of. It arrived in under a minute and he took the kind of swallow that said it had been a long day.

The past is illusion, the future a dream: be this moment. What could I get out of this supposed friendly meal? I glanced at his glass. "That was fast. Your reputation must precede you."

"I've done some work here."

"What kind?"

"The discreet kind. Crime's bad for business. If it happens management wants it handled double-Q: quick and quiet."

An *in* with management! "Your reputation does precede you then."

"Yeah. They're going to add *cucaracha con queso* to the menu."

131

"You'd be served with cheese?"

"I'm served with whatever I want."

I held the smile and forced myself to wait for a few beats before taking a warm bite of chowder. "So, what brings you here, Roach?"

"Another meal with you."

"Am I buying you dinner, too? No wonder men fear to be in your debt."

"Nah. This is on the house. Your debt's a whole lot more."

"In your dreams!"

Before he could react, a skyscraper of crabmeat arrived, surrounded by a forest of greens and bright yellow chanterelle mushrooms—faster than I'd ever seen food this side of take-out.

We Lotts take our eating seriously, and mere apprehension doesn't impede appetite. Serrano attacked the meat, but on the edge of the great mound—for presentation, only, I guessed—were legs. I sucked the flesh out of them, one after another.

As Leo'd said, taking the wrong road doesn't get you there faster. Consciously I didn't weigh the open roads, I kept my mind as clear as possible—the empty vessel can be filled etc. I was aware of Serrano shooting his gaze over my breasts as automatically as he passed the bread. He finished his martini and signaled the waiter without turning to see that his move was noted, but his grip was just a bit too tight on his glass. The drink arrived with the impressive speed of its predecessor.

"Tell me—" We'd both spoken at once.

"Go ahead, Declan. What esoteric secret have I uncovered that your antennae missed?"

He forked a bite of mushroom. "What was with that date of yours?"

"My date? Are you reporting back to my big brother?"

"Not likely." He grinned. "Your secrets are safe with me."

Was he actually flirting? "Macomber Dale? Got me."

"Why'd he attack Adamé?"

"You were standing right there with them. What do you think?"

"I'm *asking*." He put his fork down and leaned toward me. "What was with him and Adamé before that?"

I almost mentioned financing our production, but if the cockroach didn't know about that I sure wasn't going to be the one to tell him. "How should I know? Mac seemed to be trolling for backing—"

"Why would he do that? He's the producer; he's already ponied up, right? He's been run through an insurance check, right?"

"Look, backing's always iffy. The United States *government* almost defaulted. You can't have too much in reserve."

"But—"

"Listen, I'm going to be straight with you." I waited till he gave the slightest of nods to indicate this would make it into the register of our encounters. "I was just there to make nice. But he was there to make his own contacts. And not just Adamé. That older woman with them, she's got money, too, right?"

"Your guy was having quite a go at her."

"At some point he was telling her about me on the bridge, right?"

I hadn't been sure about that till Serrano nodded.

"The guy's a loose cannon. I live here. I've got a reputation to maintain, too." I paused. "Now you? What'd you see? Was he heavy-handing that woman?"

Serrano nodded sadly. "Yeah, I almost had to give her a hand with him."

"Really?" It was so unroachlike.

"Yeah, really!" He let a beat pass and said, "I know what you think of me, what everyone thinks. Do you suppose 'the cockroach' is accidental?

The Mission's my turf and no one crosses me. No one! You know why? So you can walk down the street at night and not get—That's why Tessa could work any hours she wanted, why she could ride that racing bike and not have it boosted out from under her. It's why there aren't shoot-outs in the streets like there are across the bay." He picked up his drink, took a small sip, but the movement shielded his face and I couldn't tell if he was really announcing the truth or giving me a cover story he'd created for himself. One he'd come to believe. "So, yeah, I could tell your *date* to get out of Harriet Knebel's face."

I ignored the Dale business this time. "But you didn't. You waited to see what'd happen. Because?"

"What do you think?"

"You wanted to see what happened to Adamé, right? How come? He's not in your turf?"

"He's in this turf." He tapped his head. "His laundering, that screws with my turf and"—he leaned closer—"he's doing deals the brass figure are above my head. When—not if—when I get him, heads'll roll like they're in a bowling alley. I've been onto Adamé ever since he and his wife moved here—over five years come January. Almost nailed the fucker twice but somehow each time he squeezed free and popped up looking cleaner than ever with me the one covered in shit. There's not going to be any third time."

"When you make the collar, you'll take the kind of step up like my becoming stunt coordinator?"

For a moment I thought that had just reminded him of our set yesterday and the hassle Mac's horn-blowing idiocy had created for him. The guy really took his image seriously! Now I realized that to him his move would be akin to my becoming not merely stunt coordinator, or second unit director. To equal his promotion I'd have to become Scorsese.

Then he produced a smile. The Mission was tough turf, as perilous as it got in this town, but for the conqueror the spoils could be huge.

Still, that was his business. Mine was Tessa. "Tell me about Ginger Rampono and the bike accident. Tessa was the cyclist, right?"

I expected him to protest or flat refuse—I didn't doubt for an instant that he'd have all the facts about his employee—but he didn't hesitate. "Right. Been on the job two weeks—"

"The job?"

"Bike messenger."

"A bike messenger," I repeated. Thinking of her whipping through downtown streets, racing up stairs to clients, grabbing deliveries, and running for her bike—it made me like her all over again. Made the horror of causing the little girl's accident all too easy to imagine. "After that, manning a copy machine . . . "

He nodded. "The accident flipped her, literally and figuratively. Over the handlebars. Landed on her head—cracked patella, severed tendon, and broken tibia. Had double vision for months."

"Oh God!" That was too close to home. "And the accident itself?"

"Standard bike-car meet-up. No clear guilt. No one charged. That's the official word. A witness said later that Tessa cut in front of the car. It caught her back wheel and sent her flying. But the witness also said the driver wasn't watching the road, talking to the little girl. When she hit the bike, she panicked, lost control . . . was killed. The kid was in the hospital for weeks." His delivery was a little off, as if he was trying for rote and failing.

Or maybe I just wanted to believe there was a little bit of "caring" in him. "And Tessa, how long was she hospitalized?"

"SF General overnight. No insurance. Signed herself out. Outpatient clinics for months."

"She couldn't work. How'd she live? Welfare? Unemployment?"

"She did what she'd done before she came here."

"Which was?"

"Shoplifting."

"Really?" He hadn't been specific before. "Minor offense" could have been check kiting or DUI. But shoplifting enough to support herself, that was a whole different animal. Particularly for a woman with a cracked knee and a broken leg. It would have been an all-day-every-day job. If that was true, copping Varine Adamé's credit card would have been a snap. And having the nerve to spend the night here with it—a breeze.

But what about the Tessa Jurovik who sent two hundred dollars—all her extra money—to Ginger Rampono? "People do hit-and-runs all the time. They don't mortgage themselves for the victim. Why'd she care so much about this kid?"

"She didn't say." He looked down at his plate for a bit, then seemed to decide to go on. "Her father walked out; her mother fell apart; and she ended up with a juvie record. She knew what this kid could be in for. It really got to her."

"But when you told her the driver wasn't paying attention—"

"I never mentioned that."

What? "You didn't tell her she didn't cause the accident?"

"She did cause it." *Mr. Logical Black-and-White!*

"But if she'd known the driver wasn't paying—"

"I didn't mention the accident," he reiterated in a case-closed tone that infuriated me. *You had to know how guilty she felt. How could you not tell her? You . . . cockroach!*

He tore off a piece of the bread.

The past is illusion, the future a dream: be this moment. I watched him . . . watched him chewing. Just chewing.

I realized why he hadn't told her.

Then I had to steel myself to keep from yelling: "That's how you met her, huh? In the cop shop. The coffeehouse bit was a lie, right? Of course you didn't tell her it wasn't her fault. You saw her record; you *owned* her. *You* set her up in a high-stress business that paid shit. No wonder she tried to kill herself."

He looked annoyed and replied in that infuriating logical-man voice. "You really get off on thinking the worst of me. So, let me tell you what happened. *She* propositioned *me*, businesswise. She'd been at the job a month. Said she knew the place was a front, knew drug deals were going down outside, and the dealers knew the place was a front, which made the whole arrangement useless."

"Except for the pleasure the dealers got laughing at you." *Good for them, you louse!*

"Yeah, right. I knew that, too. It was a problem I had to address. She came up with the answer: me bankrolling her in the specialty copy service."

I nodded, still suspicious. "So it'd be legit and you could still use it."

"Right. It'd take time for memories to fade. But even so, it was win-win."

"And you'd get to eyeball all those legal copies."

"Of course not. Do you think I spend my days looking for ways to break the law?"

Luckily I didn't have to answer that. I sipped my drink, hunting for another angle into his arrangement. But there wasn't one. Still there was something about him and what he was giving me that seemed not so much untrue as incomplete. What was I missing? The suddenly ubiquitous Mrs. Adamé, perhaps. If both Warren Llekko and Jessica Silverman had opinions about her, surely Serrano would, too. "Tell me about Varine Adamé."

"Is that what you said to the desk clerk downstairs?"

Of course, he'd asked them what I was after. "Did they also let you know that Tessa spent the night here on Varine Adamé's credit card?"

I almost laughed at his reaction. The guy was astonished, then insulted, and finally embarrassed. Then he looked as if he was seeing a section of a jigsaw puzzle clearly for the first time while shifting pieces like mad.

"Varine?" I prompted before he could get it all nailed down in his head. "Jessica Silverman said she supported some girls' charities, regularly, small amounts, low-key."

"And what a good impression she's made with that."

You really do hate Adamé. You could go snarl to snide with Warren Llekko.

I caught myself. *No past, no future, just this. Pay attention!* I said, "What do you know—"

"I don't," he said too quickly. "Adamé just uses her!" He spit the words with such outrage I almost laughed. This, from the guy who'd slapped me mere hours ago!

"She shows up at his events when she has to, but that's it. She could have a second life for all the free time she's not using."

"Does she?"

"No record of it."

"Record? Like jail? Fifty-one-fifty?"

He shrugged. For civilians a shrug is one of many choices; for a police officer it's not going on the record.

"A mental condition?" I asked in astonishment. "Why would you even—"

"Look, being married to a guy like that: it's a prison of its own. It can drive a smart woman crazy."

I lifted my glass and then put it down. Was he just projecting his own frustration with Adamé? Or was it possible he was concerned about her? Was he cockroach with a conscience?

Or did he just figure she was an easy back door to Adamé, one he could never open?

But none of this was getting me any closer to finding Tessa. "Why her? Varine Adamé? Why'd Tessa take her credit card? Where would she even— oh, shit! You! You're the connection. How did—why—?"

"Why would I do that? What's the benefit to me?"

"I don't—"

"Even for a cockroach, it's not just evil for evil's sake."

"Prove it!"

He leaned forward. "How?"

"You've done some quick and quiet work here. Get me into her room."

He considered for a second or two and then said, "Okay. What's the number?"

I could barely believe it! "Room 1701."

He laughed.

I waited.

"Room 1701, that's the Presidential Suite."

24

I'D ASSUMED SERRANO would hit up a contact in Security. What I didn't dream was that we'd arrive to find the door to the Presidential Suite already propped open.

If things went south there'd be nothing to incriminate the contact. Serrano could wriggle out of it. And I'd be out on the limb while he was sawing.

Me, trust the cockroach? Not hardly.

I walked in.

He shut the door.

"The President'd better have lots of friends," I said taking in the living room. A dining table stood to one side, doors on both sides of the room led to bedrooms, but it was the view that left me gaping. "Be hard to concentrate on the recession or Afghanistan here."

Serrano was looking down into the streets as if he owned them. But when he turned back to me there was a tightness in his face. "If you're hunting for secrets," he said, "here's a tip. Check the lesser bedroom. No one thinks to look there. If Tessa's smart, that's what she'll've figured."

Why would she have cared about hiding anything?

"And make it quick."

Uh hah! But I didn't have time to ponder the limits of his power. If there was any lead to Tessa here . . .

The second bedroom had two doubles, both turned down, both looking fresh and eager. The bathroom—pristine. I hurried back through the parlor—large, comfortable, with its killer view, but still—surprisingly—just a room. I would have thought—

A phone rang! His cell.

"Yeah," Serrano grunted. "Hey, Scatto, we had an arrange—" I heard a couple more monosyllables and a final click off. "Gotta go!" he called to me.

"Okay. Thanks."

"I mean *we* gotta go."

"What? Your contact's changed his mind?"

"Cold feet. Up and over the balls."

"I need a couple more minutes—"

"No can do. I gotta—"

"If I leave now, this is a wash."

"I have to—"

"Declan, if Tessa jumps tomorrow because we missed a lead to her here—"

He hesitated.

"Go! I'll take my chances."

He sighed. "If you end up in jail I don't know you."

Big surprise!

The door all but clanked behind him, leaving me, essentially, a burglar with no clear idea what I was after.

Still, no one's more romantic than a San Franciscan. And me, who'd been exiled for well over a decade before coming home this year, I couldn't resist turning off the lights and walking to the window. From here, the highest point downtown, I could see the bay, the Bay Bridge, Oakland, Berkeley, and beyond to the hills. Lights glowed from high rises, sparkled off the cables between the bridge towers, flowed from headlights and burbled from taillights, and disappeared as cars slowed then vanished into tunnels. I felt overflowing, overwhelmed, as if the magnificence of the view was more than one person could handle. I wanted to call all my friends to come. I wished I still had a lover to melt against as we looked from the black water to the sparkling lights.

Still, Tessa . . . How could she not have called—

What made me think she hadn't?

I called Security.

A woman answered.

"Scatto was getting me a printout of the phone records for seventeen oh one. I thought they'd be here by now."

"Your name?"

Name? Not mine! I couldn't use Serrano's. "Varine Adamé, of course. I don't want to complain, but I have been waiting." I held my breath. Would she even question me or was there a goon squad already heading up here?

"I'm sorry, but we've a situation on three that's going to take—"

"Of course," I said. "I understand. But this is a situation of some urgency."

"I don't—"

"Just the call list. Please."

"But—"

"My husband is, right now, being honored at City Hall. Of course I'll tell him about your help when he gets here." I paused to let that settle in.

It was a moment before she said, "Here're the numbers. You ready?"

I scrambled for a pen and copied down one local and a long distance number at an area code that told me nothing. "That it, just the two?"

143

"Yes. Oh, and, Mrs. Adamé, I see here there's still a question about your plans. Will you be checking out in the morning or would you like to move to another room? We do have another party coming in."

Tessa never checked out! She could be unlocking the door right now! I'd scoured the city and she'd been right here all along! She could walk in any minute and—

"Mrs. Adamé?"

"Yes, tomorrow. I'll be leaving. But I don't want to be disturbed tonight."

"No, certainly not. Have a good night."

She was still here! I was so relieved, so excited. She'd be okay. Whatever her problems, we could handle them. Now the worst possibility—I wanted to laugh—would be the one Mike had thought of, that I might bring her to dinner.

But where was she? Was she still planning to jump? She could have rented—hell, stolen—a car and be doing a farewell drive around the city. She could be down the hill in Chinatown gorging herself on delicacies that usually require a party of four to finish, or sipping noodle soup slowly in a spot below sidewalk level. She could have just decided to go to the movies.

I looked around the living room, checking around the furniture, between the seat cushions and, in the dining area, scanning the floor. Nothing.

But she was still a guest here. There had to be something.

Unless she just didn't bother to check out. Was I looking for detritus of her night before the bridge—or was I on the hunt for a sign she'd be back? That's what this room needed to tell me.

The phone rang. Again! The hotel phone, this time. Who knew I was here? Whoever was on the other end—Serrano, someone from Security— no good would come of answering.

According to Serrano's theory, if secrets were to be hidden in the lesser bedroom—and they weren't—then there should be nothing in the main bedroom but a king-sized bed. I pushed open the door.

It looked like a hurricane had hit. Sheets, blankets, comforters had been flung into swirls on the floor. More bedclothes than seemed possible to have covered one bed. The bed was down to the mattress cover. Broken glass glistened like white-on-white ornaments a couple feet from one of the bedside tables.

What in hell had happened here? I leaned back against the wall, unwilling to step farther, as if the clumps of sheets still held her misery, as if the luxury of this room merely increased the irony, the huge bed her aloneness.

I edged to the closet. She'd had the bike with her. That's what the desk clerk told me. She'd ridden it the night before she tried to jump. Now her Spandex biking clothes were here but the bike itself was gone. She'd've changed for the bridge. So now, she, in her white shirt and black pants, along with the bike, was out there somewhere.

Omigod. Was that a knock?

But not Tessa! She'd have a key.

A voice called something I couldn't make out.

Hide?

Hide? Or bluff? What was my best option?

Now I needed to make every half-second count. I waded through the sheets to the bedside table, scanned around it for anything that might have dropped.

Another knock.

I headed to the far side of the bed; the sheets were like quicksand.

I could hear the door opening.

I made for the doorway where at least my ankles wouldn't be cuffed with cloth. Options for handling Security flashed and were gone. I walked slowly into the living room.

"Room service!"

Did Security really expect me to fling open the door for that old ruse? The lock clicked. The door opened.

He wasn't what I'd expected. Not a burly guy with a burly gun. He was holding a large tray with two layers of metal dish covers. He had the look of . . . not a professional as much as a man who knew the ropes and had climbed over them, or under them, often enough to end up entangled, but was clever enough, always, to step free. He was thin in a forgot-to-eat way, mid- to late twenties, dark, gorgeous, and surprised. "Oh, I am so sorry," he said in a vaguely French accent. "Please excuse. I thought that she . . . They said she had not checked out. I wanted . . . Please excuse."

"You wanted?" There was more than just meal delivery going on here.

"I am sorry. I will—"

He was looking past me into the bedroom. He was inching away. I shot around him and shut the door to the hall. "I'm not going to report you. I'm her friend. Trust me. If she had this good a night here, I'm happy for her." I *was* happy for her. And relieved.

He shifted the tray. It must've weighed twenty pounds.

"You can put it down. Help yourself if you're hungry."

"I'm not allowed to stay—"

"Oh, please! Two glasses, silver for two, food enough to keep you till sunrise." I couldn't help but grin. "And isn't that a bit of cream on your lips? Is it standard procedure here for room service to double as food tasters?"

I expected him to protest, but he offered the kind of smile that invited me into the conspiracy. He was, I suspected—but no, I couldn't afford to stereotype him. How often had Leo stopped me mid-sentence with the question: Do you *know* that? How often had he said: Don't assume. I went with what—Marc, his pin said—had said. "You're expecting her back?"

"Expecting? No. I expect nothing."

Was that his philosophy or his answer? "What did she say?"

"About today? Nothing. She . . . but you are her friend? She gave you her key. You are meeting her, yes?"

"Not exactly."

He leaned back against the wall and eyed me in a way that said we were on level ground now. He didn't glance at the debris of the previous night behind him.

The head of Security might open the door any moment. I reconsidered Marc's opening statement. "Were you expecting her to be here or not? It's kind of hard to tell. You were surprised to find me, right? I don't blame you."

He considered for a minute. "Why do you—"

I shook my head. "You first. Then I'll tell you. Was it something she said?"

"No. She said almost nothing. I was here till sunrise. I thought I'd be fired but—" he shrugged. "All those hours, we hardly spoke. We"—now he looked toward the bedroom—"but not all night. We ate. She was not like others. I have seen the rich, the ladies with credit cards they will not have for long, *les femmes vengeresses*. They order the most expensive. Their goal is to go through money like . . . " he snapped his fingers. "They rip the sheets, they spill, smear, stomp caviar into the upholstery. They wish to destroy. But she," he said wistfully, "was not that way. She wished to savor. She'd ordered the best of everything. She tasted each bite, each sip. We did not finish the bottle. She left"—he smiled—"a tip of such size the maid was afraid to take it."

"She said nothing about the next day?"

"Only that she wished it would not come."

"How so? Romantically? Fearfully?"

"*Comment?* She said there was something she had to do. Unavoidable, that was the term she used."

"Unavoidable how?"

Something bumped the hall door. Marc went stiff.

"How?"

He was getting nervous. But so was I. I was in a lot more danger than he. "Unavoidable how, dammit?"

"A contract. She tried to break it, she couldn't." He hoisted his laden tray.

"What kind of contract?"

"She couldn't escape it. She had to go—"

The door started to open. The suit behind it couldn't have been anything but Security.

I've been in a lot of action movies; I know the options for the cornered: discuss, divert, destroy. Discuss is fine if you've got a chance of talking the big guy out of hitting, cuffing, or killing you. Which I did not. The guy in the doorway didn't fill it, but he had a look that said he'd know all the answers before I could think up the questions. Destroy him? Not hardly. Which left only one option. I was sorry but . . .

As the door opened I grabbed the tray out of Marc's hands, tipped it onto Security, and ran for the stairs.

25

IN MOVIES HEROES confuse and elude capture by running not down, but up the stairs. But there wasn't much "up" from here. I went down. I've choreographed enough stair fall gags to know how to stay upright and move fast in high heels. I grabbed banisters, whipped corners, and all but skipped the landings.

After four flights I checked the hall, stepped out, made my way along till I came to a distant staircase, and continued down. I was small potatoes, to be corralled to pay for china and effrontery. Still, I didn't leave the stairs at lobby level. I kept on going and ended up wandering through the basement and out onto the street through the garbage bins.

I'd go home, change my look, and figure out how to monitor Tessa's possible return. I couldn't bear the idea of her walking into the lobby and my not knowing.

From Nob Hill cable cars go in all directions—every one but mine. The zendo wasn't far, but the walk straight down in spike heels was plenty long enough. A lesser woman would have tipped onto her snout. I cut through Chinatown, up Grant Avenue. The sidewalks were empty. Shadows turned dark to black. I was relieved when I reached Pacific and turned right toward home, across Columbus.

Cars shoot down this wide one-way thoroughfare, whipping through lights to swing toward one of the approaches to the Bay Bridge. This late, if they're going out of the city, they're going fast. Columbus is too wide to make a dash across it. My feet ached but I made myself stop and check.

I let a single van pass and was just about to start for the zendo when I spotted the vehicle pulling up outside it. A black unmarked car.

It could have held my brother John. But if he was going to nag about the rhubarb pie, he'd do it by phone—again.

Which left Declan Serrano.

The guy could only be trouble.

I waited.

He turned off the lights and sat.

I could have kicked him. It would have eased the pain in my feet.

Get out, you cockroach! Don't just sit there!

The wind, which I hadn't noticed when I ran out of the hotel and hurried down the hill, now iced the sweat on my neck and slid under the collar of my inadequate coat.

Don't just sit there in your warm car.

I moved into a doorway and peered out at him.

He started the engine.

I let out a sigh of relief.

But the lights didn't come on. He was just running the heater!

I picked over my options like avocadoes in the deli section. When they're all too hard, you take the softest and just hope for the best. I pulled out my phone and dialed Macomber Dale, hoping he'd calmed down since the ruckus he'd caused at City Hall. Hoping he wasn't in the cop shop waiting to be booked.

"Dale here."

"Hey, Mac, it's Darcy Lott. I need a ride to pick up the junker for tomorrow's shoot. I'm freezing on a street corner." I had a hundred things I wanted to ask him, but not at this moment.

In seven minutes flat he was at the curb. Declan Serrano was still parked in front of the zendo.

"Thanks," I said as I slid in, kicked off my shoes, and stuck my feet against the heater vent.

"Sure." He pulled away from the curb. "Where we going?"

I gave him the cross streets and directions.

His only response was to veer left toward the Embarcadero and roads south. He was peering ahead like driving took all his concentration. I applauded that—good for traffic; good for eliciting straight answers.

"Mac, what happened with Aaron Adamé tonight?"

"I don't know."

You don't know? "Mac, you shoved the guy—the guest of honor!"

"I did not!"

What! "I saw you! Half the city saw you. You and I were supposed to be there tonight to make nice and we're sure not—"

"That's what I was doing. We were talking movies, Adamé and Harriet Knebel and me. I was talking up the movie, talking up you, telling him about the stunt driving and how you even saved a woman from jumping off the bridge. Saving a life, you can't get nicer than that! I know how to deal with these arty types. I've cut deals. I was working them. And then, bingo, he's pushing me aside and suddenly everyone's on me."

"You didn't touch her? Harriet Knebel?"

"What do you think I am? She's an old lady!"

"You're saying *he* shoved *you?*"

"Damn right! The asshole!"

"And then?" I was glancing at the passenger side rearview.

"He went racing out like there'd been a bomb scare. When I caught up with him he was standing outside and suddenly I'm taking the rap. Like they all thought I'd attacked him!"

I took a deep breath, but it didn't calm me down much. "Maybe what you're saying is the whole truth, but you're used to getting what you want and getting it pronto—"

"*He fucking* shoved *me!*"

"Pull over." We were a block away from the garage.

He eased to the curb. "Did I pass?"

"What?"

"Focusing in turmoil, like you told me! Couldn't've done better yourself, right?"

"What you just told me, was that true?"

"Sure, but—"

"Be at my place at 9 o'clock tomorrow." I slammed the door and Dale shot off down the empty street. I stepped back into the shadow of the nearest building before crossing to the garage.

Just in time to see Declan Serrano's car whip by.

I laughed. I wished I could catch the scene when the cockroach pulled Macomber Dale over. Who'd be the most outraged?

But by then I'd have the junker out of the garage and be out of the Mission.

26

THE GARAGE, KNOWN in the family as the mouse hole, was a shabby and cluttered box pressed between bigger commercial boxes that may have changed owners, made, sold, or stored different stuff over the years. There were no visible signs, not even subtle indicators by the mail slot, as to their current incarnations.

Mom and Dad had had a flat across the street before John was born. They'd kept a car here. When they moved out to the Avenues—a mile from Sea Cliff but hundreds of thousands of dollars beneath it—they passed the rundown garage on to a brother-in-law, and he, later, to another relative and, somehow, back to us. After a while the mouse hole had become not a convenience but more like a grumpy cat in a household that once had had mice. We kept it no matter how inconvenient because you never know.

Inside was the junker—the stunt car—next to stacks and jumbles of stuff various Lotts deemed worthy of keeping. The car was pointed out.

Odd.

Oh, wait, one of the film techs had worked on it this morning and parked it. A guy more considerate than any of us Lotts.

From habit I glanced under the hood, drove out, locked the garage door—not that anyone with any small bit of ambition couldn't get in—and headed south out of the city.

Considerate parker or not, the tech had left the car with a new squeal, the kind of thing a conscientious driver would take in to his mechanic and a junker driver just hoped didn't erupt till the heap was in the wrecking yard. (There actually was a tow lot/wrecking yard a couple blocks from the mouse hole, an arrangement that had benefitted both wreckers and Lotts over the years.) I was moving slowly, watching the cross traffic, checking the rearview.

I swung by Mom's house. No one was home, but Mom keeps a closet of emergency clothes for her offspring in need. We take; we leave. I left my cocktail dress and grabbed a plain black one, sandals, and an old leather jacket I'd gotten a deal on in an L.A. resale shop. It'd been years since I'd seen it. My hair I pulled back in a twist so tight I was almost looking at my ears. If Aaron Adamé was home too, he might still recognize me but his first thought wouldn't be: the woman with the guy who attacked me.

Sea Cliff is an anomaly in San Francisco, a couple block residential loop preserved between big segments of the Golden Gate National Recreation Area, a spot so exclusive many locals have to look at a map to find exactly where it is. It could be a bit of Scarsdale or a wealthy Chicago suburb with a view of the Golden Gate. Substantial homes sit in the middle of substantial lawns. Grass in San Francisco is like evergreens in Miami. I wondered if these folk had to send their gardener out of town to learn how to mow.

In pretty much any other neighborhood, houses were right behind the sidewalks. Here, though, there were walks leading up the inclines to the doors. Here, unlike in other neighborhoods, cars were not bumper-to-bumper by every spot of curb. I eased the car near the Adamés' walk, closed the car door, not surprised that it no longer locked, and headed to the door, rang the bell, and waited. Inside, there was a dim glow. No car was visible, but it was likely in a garage behind.

The outside light came on. The door flew open and Aaron Adamé rushed forward. "I was worri—" He stared at me. "Who the hell are you?"

"Darcy Lott. Is Varine here?"

"No."

I glanced at my watch. Almost 10:00 AM, not late certainly, but late to be just out. "Where is she?"

He looked puzzled and it was a moment before it struck me that I'd sounded concerned. I'd sounded, I realized, like a friend who'd been expecting to find her home. I'd played this role, or close to it, with Kristi; was I slipping into it all too readily now? Me, the phony friend?

I scrunched my shoulders. No need to *pretend* shivering out here. It was plenty cold. "I really need to see her. I can wait or come back. I know it's late, but this is important."

He hesitated. Up on the dais, in his elegant suit, he'd looked older and more imposing. Now, in jeans and a navy World Cup sweatshirt, he barely resembled the descriptions I'd heard: mover, dynamo, financial visionary with guts. He'd been described as leading the leading edge but now he just looked edgy and so tired I was almost sorry to be keeping him standing up. For an instant he even seemed to have forgotten I was there. Finally, he asked, "How is it you know her?"

"Through Jessica Silverman."

"Ah, yes. You better come in. It's cold."

It wasn't much warmer inside. The place would be a bear to heat. The entry was about the size of Mom's living room, but there the similarity stopped. The first thing you noticed at Mom's was the clutter on the hall table. Here there were two narrow ones, but no mail, keys, newspapers, notes, much less, and underneath, an array of shoes abandoned by whoever was living there. It was a room to walk through, as, a glance suggested, was the living room.

"When do you expect Varine back?"

"I . . . I don't know."

"Is she okay?"

"Yes. Probably." He was moving like a remote-controlled model car on low battery. Everything about him suggested his normal speed was snappy, and even now, worn out as he obviously was, he started each step with a burst but faded before his foot hit the floor. He seemed surprised to find himself in a much smaller version of the living room, dropped onto a red loveseat, and motioned me to the one opposite.

This little room was set up to be cozier, with bookcases, pictures, an electric fireplace that could have warmed but wasn't turned on, and a bar caddy from which he did not offer me a drink or take one.

I sat. "She's *probably* okay? You don't know where she is?"

"You know how she is."

"Yes and no. I mean, I'm not married to her. But you seem worried."

He shrugged.

The last thing I wanted to bring up was the reception, but I had little choice. I euphemized: "I heard comments about her skipping the award ceremony tonight."

He sighed. "Don't people have anything better to gossip about? Don't they . . ." He sighed again, longer this time. "It's always like that, people *expecting* her to be here, to be there, like she's my boutonniere. She's entitled to her privacy, her own life. She goes above and beyond and still people expect her to be everywhere! Why should anyone care if she held a glass of wine and shouted over the din tonight?"

"You *were* being honored."

"I'm honored a lot. That's what money gets you. Look, I don't mean to sound like a jerk. But people talk, no matter what. It just makes it hard on Varine."

"And you?" I was going to have to roll the dice here. How far could I go without blowing my cover? "Aaron, if this—her not showing up to-night—was nothing out of the ordinary, you'd be saying that. It's pretty obvious you're worried."

He hesitated—and he had the look of a man who never vacillated. Finally, he leaned forward, elbows on thighs, and looked directly at me. "I just hope I haven't put her 'on display'—what she calls it—too much. She doesn't drag me to the Mission, to her studio and, before, I never asked her to get involved in my work. But when I started doing well, there was pres-sure we hadn't expected. One local columnist actually told her that either she became part of my entourage, so to speak, or soon her absence would be the story and her private life would be gone altogether. I was naïve. I couldn't protect her. Of course Varine knows how much my career means. So, we kept trying to come up with the most she could get away with. But . . . it just never ends, does it?" He slumped.

"Maybe she's at her studio."

"No! I called."

"Not answering the phone?"

"How am I supposed to know? You're her friend, but don't tell me she always returns your calls. It's not like her. Maybe she didn't—"

"How long since you've seen her?"

"How long? Not yesterday. Maybe the day before. She was here; I was gone all day, till late, and then I had some guys over late and I just stayed down here. She's a lousy sleeper."

"But in the morning?"

"Gone." He shrugged. "I went out for a run and when I got back she was gone. No message. I knew she'd be at her studio."

"It seems . . ." I was hunting for a euphemism for distant relationship. "I don't know her that well, but I have to ask, is that normal?"

"Hey, it's how we live. She's an artist. She's off in her studio thinking color and shapes and designs. I'm into money and being part of this city. See, your reaction is exactly the problem."

"Sorry. I didn't mean to—"

He shook off my apology.

"You don't have any idea where she is?"

"She's always . . . gotten in touch."

"Always, before you started to worry?"

"Of—I don't know. No, yeah, okay, there was another time she was gone for almost a week, so maybe—" He nodded as if reassuring himself. "This is between us, right? I don't want to be reading about it somewhere."

"Of course." I shifted to almost face him. "How'd she seemed recently? Have you noticed changes?"

"I shouldn't be telling you this. Varine's very private."

"It's okay." I knew I should have said: *you can trust me* or *I won't repeat it*, but concerned as I was about him, still, I couldn't bring myself to lie so totally. If any word he uttered was any help in finding Tessa, no way could he trust me.

But my assurance was enough for him. "I guess you could say she's moody," he said.

"Do you mean depressed?"

"She's never been hospitalized, but there are periods she's got to be alone. I don't press her."

Never hospitalized? It was a pretty low standard. "Don't you worry?"

"Yeah, I worry. How about all the time? Don't you get it—there's nothing I can do. I've got so many meetings and crises, I can't keep up with her, with how she's holding up."

"But—"

"What am I going to do, commit her?"

"What *are* you going to do?"

"Now? I was hoping when the doorbell rang . . . She could be in a hotel."

The hotel! The *hotel!* "Aaron, that's what I came to tell her. Her credit card was used for a room at a hotel. The Presidential Suite."

"She's there?" He let out a thunderous sigh and sank back in the sofa.

"Wait. I don't know. I have to think a minute."

"I'll call—"

"They'll tell you she checked in. With a bicycle."

"A bicycle!" He shook his head. "That's so like her, a bicycle in a Presidential Suite! Riding from bedroom to bedroom." He looked straight at me. "God, I was worried, really worried this time. I . . . Shit, I am *so* goddamned relieved! You know, she could've called. We could've had— doesn't matter. Let's go."

"Wait. I'm not saying she's there."

"Then what?"

"Someone using her credit card is there."

He hesitated, then shook off the whole idea as if I hadn't spoken.

"Let me see a picture of her."

"What are you talking about? You're her friend! You know—"

"Show me the picture!"

"Behind you, on the shelf there."

I turned, reached for the frame, stopped dead. "Omigod!" There she was, standing beside him, her dark hair sweeping down beneath her chin line as it had been on the bridge. She was wearing the red drum major's jacket I'd hung on to to haul her back over the railing. I pulled the picture closer. "Omigod! This is *Varine?*"

"Of course."

"Does she have a twin?"

"No! She's an only child." He snatched the frame out of my hand. "Just what is this? Who the hell are you?"

"I'm trying to find—"

"Leave! Just get out!"

"I—"

He grabbed my shoulders. "Out!"

"Things could be easier if I went with you." He didn't object, which kept me from pointing out that only I knew which hotel we were headed to.

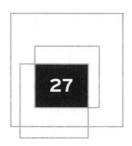

27

ADAMÉ WASN'T PLEASED about going with me, much less having to follow me to the mouse hole to drop off my car for Mac, but like any successful businessman he knew how to make deals and act nice. Declan Serrano notwithstanding, nothing about Adamé suggested he was a big-time financial criminal. But then there's a reason confidence men are called *confidence* men.

But, behind the wheel, he transformed. It was as if all the energy he'd restrained waiting for his wife exploded there. He was on my tail, blinking the lights and motioning when there was a space in the other lane, shooting over without me and slamming brakes to crawl back in behind me. The guy was so close to nudging my bumper it was almost an insult. I kept having to remind myself he was desperate to find out about his wife.

We hit a red. I was grateful. What I needed was to figure out what the hell was going on.

Behind me he tapped the horn. When I turned he gave a little "I'm here" wave. The light changed and I moved behind a truck and settled a car length back.

Varine Adamé in the hotel? Using her own credit card? *Duh!* Could *Tessa Jurovik* be an alias of Varine Adamé? Varine who had a studio in the Mission, like Tessa. Varine who craved a life of her own!

Was Tessa Jurovik merely a long-time alter ego? Was that even possible in a city this size?

I couldn't adopt an alter ego; I'd be spotted before the day was through. I'd grown up here. But a woman like Varine who'd only been here five or six years, whose public identity was in the shadow of her husband's—

I got out my cell and called the authority. Luckily, he picked up right away. "Mike, if you were less strikingly handsome and had fewer siblings prowling around the city, could you have created an alter ego here?"

"Me, sure! A lesser man, or woman maybe but . . . You mean the woman on the bridge?"

"How'd you—"

"Who else?"

"Yeah. I think she's really Varine Adamé, wife of Aaron. The red jacket, Mike, it's hers. I just saw her in it in a photo."

"One of a kind?"

"Point taken. But—"

"Are you sure she's the woman on the bridge?"

"Same hair, same clothes. But it was a studio portrait, the kind you put in a Christmas card. She's relaxed and smiling. Her husband's arm is around her shoulder. She's not frightened, angry, cold, and snarling at me. So, yeah."

"From last Christmas?"

"Dunno." I knew I needed to look for flaws in this match. "I found *Tessa Jurovik* from her pay stub."

"Just means some woman earned a salary."

"But she was a bike messenger."

"Just means some woman rode two wheels. Darce, you ride through the streets and disappear. No one checks the rolls of every messenger service in town."

Despite everything I was smiling. This was like the old days, the two of us running a single thought—usually *his* thoughts that he was willing to share with his kid sister. I'd just about killed myself to make my mark on them. Even now, driving, I could feel the tension from pressing my back against his bedroom wall, my teenaged arms around my knees, me plucking "takes" and rejecting them as too childish, worrying that I was letting the silence settle like a stain on the fabric of my acceptance.

There'd been safe but obvious comments; I'd disdained them. Maybe I'd learned early on or maybe I just knew that the only route was the most audacious, the one that would bring the supreme reward of a surprised look that said: You're not a kid anymore. Back then, like now, he'd start talking mid-idea, or I would. Now it was me: "If Varine Adamé created an alter ego in the Mission—Tessa Jurovik—and used it for a quiet life there, low-key, no one from her life as Aaron's wife would catch on. Possible?"

"Possible."

"But?"

"For her, it's not going to be so hard. It's playacting."

"But—"

"Hang on, Darce, 'cause this is the clincher. Taking another identity's only a problem when people are looking for you. Her, she's just playing at this other life, right?"

"Yeah, maybe."

"Yeah—definitely. You figure she's got this hideaway life in the Mission, to get free of the pressures of her other life. When nobody's after you, then, look, you screw up and something doesn't compute, people figure you're flaky or you've got some trouble with a guy, right?"

Toss in the night at the Mark, with Marc, the sexy bellman, and it made a pretty complete package. "Yeah, a guy. That was Kristi's first guess for pretty much anything. She liked Tessa—"

"Because?"

"Because Tessa was nice to her." There was a swishing sound on the phone, him, I was sure, nodding knowingly. "And her roommate, Byron, sheesh, she could have carried a grenade launcher on her shoulder and he'd never have noticed. He had no idea whether she was there or not. The land-lord—the landlord, Mike, he's an amateur bagpiper!"

"Say no more! Arrangement like that, *I* could have lived there and never been caught."

"Caught" was an odd word for a brother we'd been desperate to find because we loved him. Or maybe he didn't mean us. In which case—

"What's hard," he said as if continuing a thought he'd neglected to speak out loud, "is when the people who are looking for you for the best of reasons get close enough to blow your cover. Then you've got to scramble, watch your ass, and make sure you don't get them caught in the middle."

Middle of what? "You talking 'me'?"

"You once."

"You know I would never, ever have done anything to endanger—"

"Hey, you don't have any idea what agony it was to know one of you was a breath away and all I could do before I split was make damned sure there wasn't a trace you—especially you—would connect to me."

I couldn't deal with that at all. Certainly not now. I said, "But you're back now."

Behind me, Adamé flicked his headlights.

I'd slowed without realizing it. "Mike, I'm almost at the mouse hole to drop the stunt car. Varine's registered at the Mark Hopkins. Adamé's taking me—"

"The husband?"

"Yeah. He's not happy about it, but it'll be okay. Hey, wait, we're so busy trying to figure out whether or not Varine had a second life, whether it was she who checked into the hotel, I almost forgot about the bridge. All this would mean it's Varine Adamé who tried to jump."

"Yeah," he said in a what-else-is-new tone.

Why was it such a shock? There was something else, something deeper gnawing at me. "To me, Tessa's life began on the bridge. It's always central to who she is. But Varine Adamé's got a whole entire other life. For her, Tessa's like an extra cocktail dress in the back of the closet."

Mike, of course, hadn't seen her on the bridge looking longingly when a horn beeped. He hadn't been the one pulling her back over the railing. Now, to accept that Tessa had never existed except as an alias . . . it was like she *had* jumped! "To me, it was Tessa, not Varine, who was real." I had to swallow before I could trust myself to speak. "But why give away all of her clothes?"

"Clothes for her Tessa persona. Why not? She was going to jump."

"I guess."

"Darce?"

"Yeah?"

"What are you expecting to find at the hotel?"

"She didn't check out. So, with luck, her."

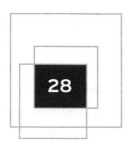

28

OUTSIDE THE MOUSE hole, Adamé flung open the passenger door of his BMW X6 and I slid in.

There was a lot he might have asked me about his wife's last couple days, but he hadn't. Not so far. Now he jumped lights before they turned green—not so unusual in this city—and ignored yellows. He ran one red entirely, and on the couple that turned half a block away, he hung rights and made sure he got through at the next intersection. The car never stopped until it jolted still by the doors of the Mark.

The first thing I noticed inside was the Security guy. Would he recognize me without my flashy cocktail dress and spike heels? I hoped—

But it was his job not to be fooled this easily. Before he could utter an accusing word, I said, "Mr. Adamé's here to see his wife, in the Presidential Suite. Can you let him in or—"

"Scatto, Security," he announced to Adamé, after shooting me a puzzled look. He had little choice but to play along. "Perhaps you'd like me to call ahead, sir."

Adamé nodded. "As you wish." He was striding to the elevator. Scatto and I followed.

"I'm afraid I owe the hotel for some breakage. Can I get a bill from you, or should I take it up with the concierge?" I said as Scatto watched his phone ring. The man had more important things than me to worry about. I'd have to pay, but now my behavior no longer counted as hooliganism, but rather the exuberance of the well-connected.

In the elevator, Scatto clicked off and then tried again. At the door he knocked, announced "Security," and then opened it.

Adamé burst in. "Varine? Are you here? Varine?" He was in and out of both bedrooms before the elevator door shut. "Not here. Empty. Are you sure this is the right room?"

The place had been restored to order. Housekeeping had been and gone. Clearly, there was no stopping the gears of a first-class hotel like the Mark. I checked the closets: no clothes, no bicycle. "Mr. Scatto, have her belongings been removed?"

"Not by our staff."

"You sure?"

"Of course. When you are a guest at the Mark Hopkins, your room is your home. We do not invade your privacy."

I walked into the president's bathroom, and leaned against the newly cleaned counter. "Why would your wife come here and rent this suite?" I asked Adamé.

He eyed Scatto and lowered his voice. "She does what she does. I don't question her."

"But—"

"Mr. Scatto, my wife and I share the credit account. So, in truth, this is my room."

Scatto took the hint.

When the door shut after him, I followed Adamé to the living room.

He was standing in front of the window, not looking out, but leaning against the glass, as if fear of the glass breaking and the resulting endless fall into the dark had no hold on his subconscious. And yet, he was clearly uneasy. Maybe keeping his back to the dark unknown was his way of handling it.

"So, why?" I prodded. *Your version, at least.*

"Varine has always had moods. She's charming when she has to be. But she needs her privacy. It's just her way. I love her. I accept that." He paused so long I thought that was it. But then he added, "I've seen her sit staring out at the fog for . . . quite a long period. Sometimes she goes from room to room and when I ask her what she's looking for she says, 'Nothing.'"

"Sounds like she has something troubling her. Did that ever occur to you?"

"She wouldn't have wanted me poking . . . ."

"So you didn't try to find out what was going on? You were honoring her need for privacy?"

"If she'd said she was depressed, of course we would have talked it out. If she'd needed medication, of course . . . but she didn't. She just . . . lived as she did." He was turning his head slowly, almost hypnotically, from side to side, as if his body itself was admitting he couldn't deal with this.

"Are you sure?" *As little thought as you've given to her!* "What about if she was desperate?"

"Why should she be?"

"Why should she be poised to take a leap off the Golden Gate Bridge? I've been trying to get a lead to the woman I pulled back from there and it's beginning to look like it's your wife."

"That makes no sense."

"Sense! We're not talking theory! I hauled her back! She said she'd try again. Maybe that's what she's doing right now." I wanted to grab him by the shoulders and shake him. "You can't just deny . . . "

He closed his eyes, then opened them. In a low voice he said, "I don't know. Maybe. Maybe she really is depressed. Maybe more lately. She says she's fine, just needs space. I guess it's been easier for me to believe her, to let her do her own thing. And there's always the excuse, *my* excuse, that I was trying to protect her, not expose her to all the constant pressure of my life. Letting her alone's been my way of respecting her. She's not fragile—I don't mean that—just fed up with crap demands. I understand that."

"Crap demands?"

"All those outstretched hands. She said it was like walking down Market Street being '*spare change*'d with each new person. Just subtler. Everyone needs donations, all good causes, like Jessica Silverman with her endless parade of pitiable little girls. Varine'd be a wreck when she got home. How could she say no, with my money there endlessly replenishing itself? That's what she told me. No way to say no, and no gift ever enough."

"Couldn't she—"

"Don't you get it? She feels trapped! Whether she actually is or not, that's how she feels! The pressure's driving her crazy!"

I remembered the tale of her diverting the food from the luncheon to the hungry people outside. And as a result, what she'd ended up with was a load of bad press. "So," I said, "was that the contract she felt trapped by?"

He looked blank.

"Aaron, there was some contract she couldn't get out of. She told—she was extremely upset about it. Upset to the point of suicide."

"Contract? *Contract?* So there really is one? I thought that asshole was just shaking me down!"

"Whoa! What contract, with who?"

He stared, as if trying to figure me out.

I stared back.

"Don't play the innocent! I saw you walk in with him. It's your movie he's backing."

170

"*That's* the contract, the deal with Dale? Why would she be so unnerved by that?" It just didn't compute. "Are you sure?"

"Oh yeah! Everyone within five yards heard him ranting about Varine being in on some deal. She had a contract with him. Hadn't paid. Now she owed him big money. It was crazy, and, let me tell you, it was embarrassing. We don't ignore our obligations. I don't know what Harriet Knebel thought, but—"

"That wasn't the idea. Believe me. He was just supposed to be meeting and greeting, drumming up support for the production. Not making enemies."

"I told him—okay, not politely—to leave. That's when the guy attacked me and you know the rest."

"But why even bother with him to begin with?"

He paused as if considering. "I don't know the details. This was Varine's thing. But, Dale's father did us a good turn years ago, when it mattered. So now his clown of a son's on the skids, desperate. I know Varine—she'd figure how could she say no?"

"Still, why get so distraught?"

"I don't know! Look, I just don't know."

We were so wound up. Too many questions with no answers. The big question was Varine, her state of mind, her safety. I had to—

Without warning, Adamé clicked a number on his cell. "This is Aaron, Varine's husband. We've had an emergency. I'm having trouble reaching her. Have you seen her in the last couple days?" I couldn't hear the reply but he seemed to be steeling himself for the final admission. "Can you tell me who to call?" Then, "Let me know if you hear anything. It's important." He disconnected and punched in a new number.

I watched him repeat the sequence four times, always gracious, but crisp enough to keep the other party from gushing or questioning. Each time without success. At the end, having gotten no encouragement, he visibly sagged.

Then, as suddenly, he sprang up. "I can't sit here. I've got to . . . I'm going to her studio."

"You know where it is?"

"Of course. But I never went there, not even a drive-by. It wasn't easy, but I never let on I knew."

I had a whole bunch of thoughts about that. "I'm going with you."

We whipped down the elevator, him questioning me about the apartment in the Bagpipe Arms. The door opened onto the lobby. Adamé strode to the valet parking for his car. I wouldn't have been surprised if Scatto from Security appeared and grabbed me.

But it wasn't he.

29

"YOU ALMOST GOT me fired!" Marc was blocking my way. He was keeping his voice down, but not his anger.

"Sorry. Really. I"—it galled me to have to admit—"panicked. Anything else I did would have ended up incriminating you."

"And yourself."

"There's that. But I was incriminated anyway and I've promised to pay. So, you're in the clear." *Unless you're spotted with me now.* A nicer person might have mentioned that. Instead, I said, "We're still trying to find her. There's been no word at all. You were the last person to see her."

"Good luck."

"Wow, that's a little cold for a woman you spent the night with just yesterday."

"Yesterday is not today."

"And that means?"

He stared at me a moment, then shrugged. "Nothing. It means nothing at all."

He turned away.

"Not hardly. What changed things?" I caught his arm and held him there. "Did you see each other today?"

"I saw *her*. She . . . *she* saw a bellman."

Behind him I could see Aaron Adamé looking around for me. "What happened?"

He pulled away.

"Was she in the suite? Did she call you? What? Marc, this is a woman who's trying to kill herself!"

He inhaled slowly, straightening, the way people do when gearing up for decision or escape. "Do you see that shop over there? The mannequin." He nodded in the direction of a boutique on the far side of the lobby. Its window framed a single elegant mannequin dressed in a honey brown tweed suit that was such a period piece it took me a moment to realize it was actually for sale.

"She was dressed like that?"

"She moved quickly across the lobby to the main entrance. When she noticed me, she nodded like any other rich lady to her gigolo and kept going."

"The same woman you spent the night with?"

"The same skin and bones. Beneath the flesh, who can say? I am not often so naïve. I hoped . . . I brought the tray and . . . "

Adamé had moved to the center of the lobby, scanning the area. In a minute he'd be gone with or without me.

To Marc I said, "What about that contract she couldn't avoid? The one she talked about the night before?"

He shrugged. "Renegotiated."

"What?"

"Something changed. Enough for her to buy new clothes."

I looked over at the mannequin in the shop window, and in that moment Marc was around my side and through the service door behind him, the one I hadn't even noticed and he had been watching.

But I had more pressing concerns. I caught up with Aaron Adamé as he cleared the main entrance and made for his waiting X6. But I'm a pro.

In one smooth dive I opened the door and slid into the seat as the car shot onto the street.

There's no way to drive down from Nob Hill without qualifying for stunt pay. Adamé chose the drop-and-bounce route to the Embarcadero, crossing cable car tracks, nearly plowing through pedestrians in Chinatown, jumping lights and screeching around corners. At a light on the Embarcadero where there was no option but to stop, he said, "She'll be there," as if assuring me, as if positive thinking would make it so.

I knew it couldn't be true. It made no sense for her to buy a whole new look, not clothes she liked, but ones she could point to and purchase quickly, if she was going back to her old life.

But the bike? Did she fly down that hill, on a bicycle, wearing a vintage tweed suit and dress pumps and praying her handbrakes would hold? Or did she haul the bike into a cab for the near vertical trip, and chance leaving a trail? In fact why not jump on the bike in her biking gear and maneuver the steep hill down to Union Square? Macy's, Saks, Bloomingdale's, Neiman Marcus, they were all there, half a mile away. She could have had her pick of looks.

Oh. She'd've had to sign the credit card there. In the lobby boutique she could charge the clothes to her room. What did that tell me?

She didn't want her signature on record now.

Was it at the hotel? I'd have to find that out. Later.

Now it was all I could do to keep from being banged around like seeds in a maraca. Adamé shot through the Mission, every turn seemingly spur of the moment, every stop a near-windshield event. When he pulled up by the apartment, forbidding as the neighborhood was, I was relieved. Her building was shabby in daylight, and darkness did not improve it. The streetlight was broken and shadows coated the stucco cube like extra layers of soot.

He opened his door. "Wait here."

"No way." I was out and onto the sidewalk. "Entrance on the side." What light there was on the street didn't make it to the narrow path between buildings. I'd be stumbling over rats—alive or dead—before I realized they weren't just mounds of garbage.

Naturally, then, there was no light over the door. I rang the bell, surprised that that worked. We stood, ears perked.

"Nothing," I muttered, and proceeded to press all three buzzers.

They rang into silence. I tried the doorknob, but now when I needed it to open, it didn't budge. Of course she wasn't here. Still, I pounded again.

There was just enough light to reveal Adamé next to me shaking his head.

Behind us, on the street, I heard glass breaking.

"Damn, that's all I need! Hey, get away from that car!" He raced toward the sidewalk.

I shot a glance at the second-story window. If she was there, this'd be the time she'd be peeking out of the edge of the shade.

Nothing moved, not enough for me to make out in the darkness.

On the street, someone was yelling back at Adamé.

Jeez! Didn't the guy have any street sense? I bolted down the steps after him. I found him facing a figure about his own height, burly but shaky enough that his most potent weapon was probably his smell. Still, if you live on the streets, carrying a knife makes sense. Adamé must've had the same take; he already had his wallet out.

Or not. He wasn't handing over his entire billfold in panic. He was giving the guy a couple of bills. He was patting his shoulder. He looked like he was about to hug him.

And now he was bouncing back to me.

"That homeless guy, he saw her! Less than an hour ago. On her bicycle, riding away from here."

"To where?"

He pointed north.

Toward downtown. "Did she say she was going downtown? Or was she just headed that way?"

"He saw her, didn't talk to her, other than to ask for money."

"So she was riding downtown." Toward BART, to airport transit, to buses with bike racks. "That could mean anywhere."

But he wasn't focused on the future. "An hour ago! She was here an hour ago!" He was almost whooping. "I'm so goddamned relieved. I can't . . . I didn't realize how frightened . . . I'm just so relieved."

"But . . . ?"

"Yes, yes, I know. But she's alive; that's what matters. She could have— I have to say, now that I know she's alive the thought of that bridge turns me to stone. I can't believe . . . But she's not there. She's ridden off to . . . somewhere. Maybe home. Maybe she's home right now. Shall we—"

I looked at my watch. It was almost midnight. "Call me. If she's there, you don't want me hanging around."

He nodded.

"Call me when you get home, okay? Either way." If she wasn't there I'd ask about friends and relatives who didn't like him. If she was past renegotiating her contract, they'd be the ones she'd be seeking refuge with. With luck—with a bit of tact—I'd be the one talking to them.

"Of course," he said. "Soon as I get home."

Maybe. "Give me your cell number." The Golden Gate Bridge walkway was closed. All was good for the night. So why did I feel so uneasy?

30

Aaron Adamé dropped me back at the mouse hole to pick up the junker I'd need for tomorrow in Berkeley. In the time it had taken us to drive there he'd moved from saying Varine might have been heading home to picturing her already there, showered, wrapped in the blue and yellow Mexican bathrobe he'd gotten her for Christmas, and nibbling on the cranberry biscotti he'd left out on the table for her. He'd interspersed each comment with thanks to me. He was desperate to get home.

I was equally desperate to get a hold of Declan Serrano. I called the station.

Not in. Did I want to leave a message?

Nope. Would they give me his cell?

Not a chance.

I hesitated, drove a couple blocks, pulled over, and dialed again.

And hung up before the ring started.

A car squealed around the corner, another on its tail. This was not a neighborhood in which to be hanging around hesitating.

Do it or screw it! I redialed Mike.

"What's up, Darce?"

"Tell me if there's any way this can put you in a bind, okay?"

"You sure know how to get a guy's attention."

Without planning to I'd ended up on what I still was calling "Tessa's" street. I pulled over. "Can you get me Declan Serrano's cell phone number?"

"The cockroach! You want the personal cell phone number for the cockroach? Should I get you the devil's home phone, too?"

"Some'd say it's the same line."

Mike laughed. "Give me ten." He clicked off.

I didn't have to give him ten at this particular spot. That's why cell phones are mobile.

A car cruised around the corner and stopped.

Byron, the roommate.

And, from the looks of it, his girlfriend. Also, from the looks, he'd never have passed a Breathalyzer and he sure wasn't walking a straight line. Nor was she. I rolled down the window, as much to see if they made it to the door as anything. Byron had grumbled to me about her refusing to spend the night when Tessa was there. That told me something.

A blast of noise came from the house. The two of them started.

"Fucking bagpipe!" he yelled.

At midnight, this really was a lawless neighborhood.

My phone rang. "Mike?"

"Here you go . . . "

"Hang on." I cranked up the window. "You got it?"

"Yeah but—why're you calling him?"

"Long story. Short is, I was told a homeless man across the street from the Bagpipe Arms saw her leave. But this isn't a neighborhood where the homeless hang out. There might be SROs around. There might be alleys a guy'd sleep in. But it's not like downtown where you'd find them hanging on the street hoping for cash. So, who was this gentleman, hanging out across from the apartment of the missing employee of Declan Serrano?"

"So you're going to call him and ask?"

"I am. No reason he shouldn't tell me."

"Hey, Darce, let me know."

"Don't worry."

I punched in the number.

It rang.

And rang.

What kind of cop with cohorts on both sides of the law doesn't pick up his phone? What reason?

Many, of course, and most of them not good. If I were wont to worry about Declan Serrano, I'd be worrying.

□ □ □

The law of karma is never broken.

Actions have consequences, as I discovered after sitting morning zazen in the zendo the next day, then slipping back into bed. I'd left my cell turned off. But killing your phone is electronic deferred maintenance, deferred not so long as I'd've liked since Jed Elliot had the landline number.

I picked it up on the fourth ring. "Good morning!" I'd learned the trick of sounding alert and chipper while still half asleep.

"I left you three messages!"

"Oh shit, my phone . . ." Everyone's had cell phone problems. They don't want to know yours.

"Time's changed. We've got the Berkeley pier from nine on. Mac'll be knocking on your door at eight-thirty."

"Not a problem." How had I left things with the unreliable Mr. Dale? I couldn't remember exactly, but I was eager to get the truth from him about his involvement with Varine Adamé.

What time was it? Almost eight already? I checked messages. Besides the three from Jed there was just one: from Adamé: "She's here! She's okay! I knew you'd want to know. She's still asleep now, and . . . I'm sure you understand. So, give us a couple days alone. After that we want to take you to dinner—dinner anywhere you choose. I'll be in touch."

Call you later! That was it?

No way! I punched in his number now. There were questions I needed answered—this minute! Of course, I got his machine.

I considered calling Declan Serrano, but if Varine Adamé was, in fact, at home, there'd be nothing more he could tell me. In any case, there was no time. I did a speed shower, threw on "standard stuntwear": black pants with give, cotton, not synthetic, in case the gag goes bad and there's fire, and a high-neck black shirt with a zipper in case I ended up not needing one that warm.

After the last tension-crammed days it'd be good to have one straightforward one filled with no more than normal problems, ones I could easily handle.

I hoisted my deal-with-any-emergency work bag and headed to the corner for espresso and Renzo's morning bun with what he called his "special sauce." It was not only special to him, but special to each day. Today the crisp layers of the bun were filled with a thick pineapple paste spiced with the tiniest hit of chili. For a moment nothing else existed but the hot tangy taste. I took a sip of the coffee—a double. Per Renzo, the only reason for a single espresso was to remind you you should have had a double.

A man and two women hurried in and grabbed the table nearest the counter and, with it, Renzo's attention.

I sat, sipped, pondered Varine Adamé, and it struck me how different my feelings were for the woman I'd saved, now that I thought of her as Varine, rather than Tessa. Not that I knew either one of them! Both illusions, just one that I liked better. I'd been caught by "Tessa" and her "I did one decent thing and now you've ruined it." But as Varine, what would that one decent thing be? She was a rich woman—her problem was being asked to do too many decent things. She wouldn't have to pay with her life.

And yet what happened on the bridge happened.

One decent thing?

A horn blew insistently. Of course it was Macomber Dale.

31

"Empty!" The mouse hole, he meant. Macomber Dale stalked to the old Civic I'd parked in front of the zendo. "What was I supposed to do?" he demanded.

"What you did—call Jed." Why was he making such a crisis of it? Why had he even gone there? Had Jed . . .

"I was going to leave my car there, in the garage—"

"It's safer by the zendo, believe me. Anyone can jiggle that decrepit lock and walk right in. It's protected by its shabbiness, but only barely."

He unlocked the car and I had to scramble to get in before he was away from the curb. The guy'd been twitchy yesterday, but now he was like one of those particles in a science video springing all over its atom. His hands were shifting on the wheel, his knees nearly knocking. It clearly was not the moment to start in on his Varine connection, but it took a superhuman effort not to barrage him with questions about it. And, whose version of the encounter with Aaron Adamé could I trust? The main thing, though, was that I had to put the production first right now. *Faster!* was my ticket upward, so I resigned myself to going slower on all matters Adamé.

How had Dale ever gotten Jed to trust him with our vehicle before the shoot? In the script sequence, the shot we were setting up didn't directly follow the last scene with the car, so if Dale managed to scrape a fender it wouldn't be a continuity crisis. But anything more major would. The problem with junkers—*another* problem—is the older the car the more individual it becomes with its fading paint, ripped seat covers, mirrors jutting at angles of their own, and of course those scrapes and dents. It'd be easier to reshoot scenes than to hunt up a duplicate and poke and scrape it till it matched.

"Mac, how come Jed let you take this car?"

He looked sheepish.

Oh shit!

All five lanes of the Bay Bridge were jammed. Mac jerked from one sluggish line of cars to another.

I could've called Jed and said . . . what? *I'd just assumed . . . and now here I was paying the price.*

Mac was watching me, waiting for me to say something. The man was barely even looking at the traffic on this five-lane weave of speeding vehicles!

I had plenty of scores to settle with him, but the middle of the freeway was not the place. I waited a minute, pulled out my phone, and called my answering service.

One message: My agent needed more résumé packets. With an updated video.

I redialed Adamé. If I was going to die on this bridge I wanted answers from Varine about her contract with Mac.

But they—no fools—didn't answer.

I called Declan Serrano's cell. No answer.

Next, I tried Byron's number. Nothing there either.

By the time we got off the bridge I was every bit as frustrated as he. Three major freeways looped around and into each other. Traffic was all but stopped. We were an inch behind the car in front, with Dale playing the clutch against the gas. All the emotion of the last two days began to pour forth as I watched the guy chance wrecking our car and screwing up the shoot.

"This the way you handled Var—"

"Your guru—"

What? "My teacher? Leo?" Where'd that come from?

"Whatever." *Now I've got your attention,* his smug expression said.

Had he gone to Leo to confess? Zen priests aren't like Catholics; they don't absolve sins. But no reason he'd know that. "Leo?"

"He was carrying on about karma. I mean, like, mine's bad."

Bad karma, the flag term of the pop Zen world! Few concepts have been as distorted as karma. Still, if bad karma existed in the way Mac thought, who could be more deserving? "Bad karma? How'd he put that?" This was going to be interesting.

"Your teacher. He was going on about consequences."

"Actions have consequences?" *How many times did I have to be reminded of that today?* If Leo'd been talking to me he would have said that every action or inaction has consequences because all things are interconnected. Karma is the weave of life. But talking to Mac . . . ?

"Yeah, consequences." He was now eyeing the left lane where cars were moving.

"We get off at University, up ahead."

"Right." He shot over.

"What consequences?"

"He said if I'd thought *before* . . . But then he said *before* was gone. Only it's not exactly how. . . "

"The past is gone, the future illusion."

"Yeah, and something about a tangled web—"

All my ancient tangled karma from beginningless greed, hate, and delusion, I now fully avow. I knew the traditional chant of repentance, but what did that have to do with—

"Tangled with the stuff that happened before?" he demanded. "The mistakes I made?"

"Mistakes? With Varine Adamé?" *Mistakes about our funding?*

He cut right, managing to swing into the next lane and the next. Behind, brakes screeched. University Avenue exit's tricky; there's no easy way to get over the freeway. I could have helped him, but I didn't.

I said, "The contract you made—"

"Contracts are paper." He hung a U and headed back across the freeway. On the top of the overpass he slowed, looking ahead at the wooded roadway, the bay, San Francisco beyond. "It's the economy," he added, as if that explained everything. "Bad."

Oh shit! "*How* bad?"

"Total bad. Took a beating in the market . . . serious beating. Treading water . . . maybe. You wait for the turnaround but, sometimes, dead is dead."

"So, just *how* bad?"

He said nothing. Which said everything.

"What about the Adamés? They guaranteed—"

"Not going to happen."

"But didn't they sign—does Jed know?"

"Doubt it."

"The director, the other producers? Didn't you tell anyone?" I couldn't believe it! How could he—"We haven't been shooting that long! You must've known things were shaky. How come—"

"It's not hard to convince people your money's good."

I'd meant how come you didn't warn a single person!

We were on filled land now, here in the Berkeley Marina. The roadway was like waves. He hit every crest, nearly sending me into the roof each time.

I'd collar Jed as soon as we got to the site. He'd be on the horn pronto. Would we even do a set-up today? Was there any point? Only if the other backers could absorb this. If we blew off this shoot, even if we got the spot again a month or two from now, how much of a continuity problem would we end up with? How many actors would have other gigs? And the director, the crews? It was a nightmare.

"Hey," he protested, "I haven't done anything so terrible. What's the worst that can happen, people don't get to go to a big dark room, slobber down popcorn, and stare at a screen for a couple hours? It's not like—"

"Not like what? Not like *people* make movies? Not like *people* lose their jobs? Like vendors we contract with getting stiffed? Not like us losing cred with the city? So you were just playing us!"

"No! I wanted to be a movie producer! I wanted things to work out for once. And I thought they would this time." He sneaked a glance at me. "Things happen. Like upswings. Why not now?"

"But they didn't happen, did they? How long've you known?"

"I don't *know* now. Look, if I could have pulled this out of the fire, I would. If *I* could get out I would. You don't know what it's like always being the screw-up!"

I didn't have time for his emotional baggage. "Look, Varine Adamé gave you a guarantee—"

"She didn't *give* me anything! We had a deal and now she's not paying. She hired me—"

"To do what?"

"Hassle the cop."

"Oh, right!" I said in full sarcasm. "Listen, I'm asking you—" But, he wasn't listening at all.

"She used me. Don't you get it—no more money!"

"There's Jed. Pull over. We'll talk about this on the sidewalk!"

"Look, I—"

"Stop the fucking car!"

But he didn't. He hit the gas.

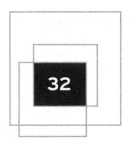

32

"Are you out of your mind?" I screamed as he shot through the intersection. "Pull over here!" I jabbed a finger toward our lighting truck on the side of the road.

Ignoring me, he whipped past it, past the bait and tackle shop, past the exit from the parking lot beside it. The rest of University Avenue was blocked off for our set-up. Mac shot around the detour sign pointing outsiders through the parking lot.

"Slow down! We've got crew here! They're not even thinking 'street.' They're thinking 'set.'"

"Fuck 'em!"

"Get a grip! They're people you know!"

He stared ahead, jaw jutting, hands clenched on the wheel. Gravel shot from beneath the tires. I eyeballed the terrain—macadam broken, tree roots erupting, underbrush composed of God knew what. Not a clear place to chance a dive.

And there was the car. We needed the car. He was driving crazy, but he wasn't losing control. The best thing I could do was wait him out. I braced my feet and brought my arm in close, ready to shield my head or catch the dashboard.

Jed Elliot burst from behind the camera cart, waving his arms.

Mac surged by him. We were next to the grassy divider. Thirty yards ahead was the other roadblock, which marked the border of our set. Beyond that was Seawall Drive.

Beyond that, the bay.

Either he'd have to turn right, or loop around the divider and head back to the freeway. My guess was he'd take the right, down Seawall, unaware it was a dead end. With luck someone had called the cops and he'd be stopped before he could do a three point and raise hell all the way back to the freeway. I wasn't worried . . .

. . . much.

But I was checking him out. No seat belt. Of course! But also no way I could reach over, open his door, and shove him out. No, my best hope—

"What are you doing?" I shouted.

He'd rammed through—not around but through—the marker horse and was shooting across Seawall. Onlookers leapt back. A few screamed. On the edge of the road, the car hung for an instant, its wheels caught on the curb, then headed down the steep incline. As if exhaling out of its balk, it whipped down the walkway toward the pier.

The pier! Not the pier! "Turn left! Now!"

A tall man was bending over a woman. Now they were screaming; we missed them by inches. To our left people were running behind the huge sundial, scrambling up on it. I needed to grab the wheel, regardless—

But I couldn't, not here.

"Don't—"

But he did. He skirted the sundial, seeming like he was about to do the sensible thing and veer back up onto the road. At the last moment he hung a sharp right onto the pier.

He was headed straight toward the storage building.

"Stop! It's a car killer!"

"What?"

No need to explain, he'd already yanked the wheel and cut around the little cement structure.

"You can't drive on here!" I yelled. "The pier's falling apart. The boards are rotten."

"Rotten, huh?"

The pier was two cars wide—two *old* cars. Mac flew down the middle. Pedestrians slammed their backs into the railing. A bald guy with a pail beside him dropped his fishing rod into the water. The pier looked like it went on forever, weathered and narrowing till it disappeared into the bay. Ahead wind snapped strands of a woman's long black hair in her open mouth— she was screaming, too.

There was a surreal feel to the whole thing. No point in demanding, threatening, cajoling. There was nothing for me to do, but wait till Mac spotted the reinforced railing at the end, slowed to a stop, and started making the seventeen-point turn it'd take to turn around.

Suddenly the end was in front: eight feet tall, thick cross beams, the kind of barrier meant to take on a speeding car.

"Stop! You're going to get us killed! Stop, now!"

He did. He slammed down on the pedal. Brakes screeched, the car rattled, gave one bounce and stopped. Jed Elliot was fussy about the brakes on his stunt cars.

"Get out!" he yelled.

We'd been outdriving my fury, but now it caught up with me full force. I was so angry I couldn't manage words. I snapped off the belt, jumped out, and slammed the door so hard it bounced back open and I had to slam it again. Then I started back toward shore at a trot. He'd nearly wrecked the car; he could handle turning it around without my help.

193

One thing was for sure—if he'd been worried about Jed exploding when he told him he didn't have the money, that wasn't going to happen. By the time Jed finished yelling about this caper with the car he'd be too deflated to explode. Then, the problem of finding new backing and renegotiating contracts and permits, and all the other hassles, would be worth it for the relief of never again setting eyes on Macomber Dale.

The pier was so long I had a half mile to cover as I headed in. The wind whipped my hair around me, fueling my outrage. And it was cold, a good ten degrees colder than I was dressed for. I had more clothes, but they were in my bag in the car. That made me angrier yet. I lengthened my stride and picked up my pace.

Behind me I heard the engine start.

I didn't turn around.

Gears ground.

No need for that. It was just going to make turning around harder. But I'd be damned if I'd point that out.

Wheels squealed.

He was backing up. Toward me.

I slammed into the railing and turned.

The car screeched to a stop five yards away.

What the hell was he up to?

He hit the gas; the car shot forward. For a moment I thought he'd slam into the barrier at the end of the pier.

I was wrong. He veered left and shot through the railing into the bay.

33

THE CAR SHOT off the pier, pancaking on the water fifteen feet beyond. Waves of mud spewed up from the bottom like brown daisy petals around it as it sank. It seemed to hover there on the water way longer than the laws of physics should have allowed.

I ran to the broken railing, waiting, expecting, to see the driver's door open and Macomber Dale pop up. There was time for that. The car was still sitting on the water. But the door didn't budge. Okay, then the window would open. I waited and watched. The car was old; the windows were manual. They were big enough for him to slip through. He could push off the seat, shoot up, and . . .

But he didn't. The car shimmied as if it weren't in the water at all but merely on a wet patch. It was still upright, hadn't flipped from the trajectory and the force of impact.

Any second the water would curl around it, suck it in, swallow it.

But not yet.

Time didn't move; it spread wide like the bay water. Time with no time line. The car was suspended in the static *now*. Like *now* had frozen time and Mac and the car and me all in it.

A gag I'd done five years ago: a cannon roll. Suddenly, I was back there, in the stunt car with the explosive canister welded to the floor. I was harnessed in behind the wheel, staring through the breakaway windshield, doing eighty, ninety, hitting the ramp, plunging the button that set off the fireworks. Metal shaking like a can full of pennies, rattling like I was one of the coins, the blast so loud it blew out my earplugs, the car shooting up, hanging forever in its own eternal now, flipping over, banging down, flipping again, eternal slo-mo. No way to control it, just hope—flip—terror—bang. Along for the ride.

I'd landed upright. The guy who tried it the next year hadn't. Hadn't walked away. I could still see his car crunched down—

I gave my head a hard shake. In the bay the junker was shimmering. "Get out!" I yelled.

Already it had floated too long. If he pushed the door open the motion would break the stasis. Enough to sink it?

What was the choice? He couldn't just sit there.

If this had been a gag we'd have had an all-crew safety meeting beforehand. There'd be a big crane squatting next to me. We'd have welded heavy metal loops on the car. The safety crew'd be in the water, hidden from camera view; the instant it went under and Jed Elliot yelled, "Cut!" they'd be grabbing for the lines, hooking them to the loops. The crane would be grinding, yanking up line, and before the driver could exhale, he'd be breaking the surface. He'd be grabbing a line to be hoisted up to the dock amid the cheers of the crew. Otherwise, the crew'd get him up pronto and into the waiting ambulance.

The car was quivering, as if it were cold. I couldn't see through the back window. Frantically, now, I turned around, stared down the pier. No one was running toward us. The pier was too long. On shore they hadn't even seen what happened.

"Mac! There's no one here! No one to help! You've got to get out yourself! Mac! Push the door open! Now!"

The car shimmied. Was he getting loose, pushing to open the door? Or was it settling?

I reached for my phone. My phone that was in my bag. My bag was—shit!—in the car.

"Mac! Say something!"

Nothing!

He should be yelling. There should be people running out the pier. Boats, windsurfers, someone! How could this be? Us alone here?

Then the car sank.

Just like that.

I stared, gauged how many strokes it'd be from the pier. I ripped off my sweater, yanked off my shoes, piled my jeans on them. I almost dived when I remembered how shallow the bay was, so shallow they had to dredge shipping channels. Shallow everywhere but under the Golden Gate. I jumped.

Shallow is relative.

I thought my feet would hit bottom and I'd push back up. They didn't. There was nothing to push against. I hung there under water for what seemed like forever—suddenly here I was under the Golden Gate, down two hundred forty feet, down farther than I could ever get back up from, bones broken, organs punctured, breathing in water, water, with no chance of, no hope, the current smacking me into—

I kicked like mad for the surface, coming up so hard I popped out to my waist, gasping, coughing, squinting to see light. I was so relieved I couldn't move, until I sank back and in panic kicked again.

"Tessa!" I yelled before I realized what I was saying. "Mac!"

"Mac! Dammit, answer me!" What was the matter with him? Hit his head? Blacked out? Floating in the coffin of the car?

Where was the junker? Water covered it. I kicked hard, pushed up, looked for bubbles. Repeating it, I looked the other way.

There! I swam toward it. The water was freezing. The air iced my wet skin. Water splashed in my eyes and I kept blinking it away. I started to yell to him again and water sloshed in my mouth.

I could see it! The front bumper was sticking up, maybe ten feet below. The car was balanced like it was sitting on its trunk. Mac was lucky, so very lucky. He'd be there in the air pocket.

As long as it lasted.

Not long in that old car, in that position. Any movement I made—or he made, especially him—could knock it off whatever it was balanced on and slam it down to the bottom. If that happened—

I took a deep breath and dove.

The water was thick, muddy still. I couldn't keep my eyes open long enough to find the door. Had to surface.

I shot up, gasped, breathed, then dove again. I forced my eyes open despite the mud and the stinging. I kept squinting. The car was to my left; I dove farther, felt for the handle on the driver's side, couldn't find it.

I could see him inside, knocked out. Floating like a corpse. His head was by the passenger door. I'd never—

I shot up, burst out gasping. My lungs burned; my eyes were blurry. They hurt. I inhaled again, headed down on the other side of the car. At least I knew the passenger door was unlocked; I'd slammed it myself.

Something hit me. Knocked me into the car. Knocked the wind out of me.

Was it him? No. Too high up. Debris, something big. A hunk of the pier?

No air! I had to surface—now!

I gasped, fighting the panic of no oxygen. I couldn't let myself—How much air did Mac have? I'd have to get him free this time. I was still gasping.

I had to get under control. *Focus!* I spent precious moments making myself focus on my breathing. When I felt my heart slow, I dove. Opening my eyes, I grabbed the bumper and pulled myself down, drew my feet down, braced them against the bumper and propelled myself toward the door handle.

The water had rushed inside since my last dive. It was up to the dashboard. Mac floated—out cold—head against the windshield.

I grabbed the handle and pulled.

The door didn't move.

I pulled again.

Nothing.

My breath was gone. I had to surface.

But I couldn't.

Pulled.

Nothing.

I shot up, gasping.

Noise. People shouting.

No time. I inhaled and went down again, going through the same maneuver again. The water was up to Mac's nose. He had only seconds! I braced my feet, grabbed the handle, and pulled.

The door sprang open.

Water rushed into the car. The car jerked, slipped fast down to the bottom. Mud shot up. The recoil flung me back.

I couldn't see the car. It'd be full of water. There'd be no air pocket at all.

Everything in my body screamed: Get air! Gasp! My lungs ached. My vision was blurring. The mud turned the world brown.

I had to—

No time!

I moved downward, frantically squinting. No chance of spotting the bumpers now. I was going by feel. I circled my hands, kicked again. My lungs compacted to stones.

Metal! The roof? I circled my arms wider.

The door! Still open! I grabbed it, pulled myself down, in between the door and the car.

Coffin of a car.

My lungs screamed.

I grabbed Mac around the middle and pulled him out, pushed off the car, and sent us up to the surface.

A woman and a guy were there, treading water. "Here! We'll take him!"

Gasping, coughing, I let him go. I felt like I was going to throw up.

Was he dead? Were they working on him? I couldn't see.

Suddenly I was shivering all over, knees pressing into chest, eyes fogged. I couldn't . . . couldn't even think.

Someone lowered a rope—the same one they'd used for Mac's body?—and gratefully I slipped it under my armpits and let myself be dragged upward like a body found floating under the bridge.

34

By the time I was lifted to the dock, an emergency vehicle—the one from the set, no doubt—had arrived and Macomber Dale'd been deposited in it. It was making an oh-so-careful three-point turn. In a few minutes the entire crew would be out here.

The sun hadn't even broken through the fog yet. It wasn't quite eleven o'clock!

"Is he alive?" I asked the cop standing over me.

"Yeah. Friend of yours?"

It took me a moment to see things from her point of view. I was still shivering despite the blanket the EMTs had wrapped around me. My head felt like it had ballooned inside my skull, making it hard to process any thought at all. Of course, she didn't know what had happened before the car went in. No one did but me. "Acquaintance. Do you have any coffee?"

She walked over to a pack and extricated a thermos. "Peet's," she said. "My own emergency supply."

Make this woman chief! "Thanks." I opened it and let the steam warm my chin. I wanted to jump inside. Sipping slowly, I pondered how much to tell her. What I needed was to get Jed out there so he could get the car hauled out, and not screw up our chance of using the location here, when and if we did do the shoot. Assuming there was still adequate backing without Mac, assuming we could get the car out of the bay. What about Dale's connection to Varine Adamé?

"Did he say anything?" she asked.

"Suicidal, you mean? It'd be a stupid way to go. And, frankly, yet another expense for our budget, not that that'd be something he'd consider."

"You don't sound very sympathetic."

I looked down at my wet cold body. "Maybe I'll learn something that will make me. But right now, I was supposed to be setting up a stunt here. We're on a tight schedule. The city's only given us this spot for a couple hours. He's wrecked the set-up, wrecked the car, and my spare clothes are in the fucking bay!"

She started to reply, then turned toward the crowd now thundering at us.

I hadn't considered Mac's moronic behavior as a suicide attempt. He might as well've used the bathtub. But now I wondered. Maybe not planned; maybe spur of the moment. Nothing I'd seen suggested an ability or even a desire to control his impulses. But, then, that was the guy's MO. Maybe—*Oh shit!*—his driving off the pier had been spurred by my mention of Varine Adamé!

I drank the coffee, and, all the while continuing to shiver, watched Jed, the camera crew, the gaffers jog out along the planks. I assured them all that I was fine. That disposed of, the issue became the car.

"We could get a crane," Jed proposed.

"It'd sink the pier *if* it could even maneuver onto it."

"Barge?" the cop suggested.

Jed stared at her like she'd lost her mind. "That'd be our whole budget."

She stared back. "Don't even think of leaving that vehicle in our waters. This is the city of Berkeley you're dealing with. We take illegal parking very seriously."

I smiled and took another swallow of her coffee, and let them work it out. Finally, they settled on a marina tow truck.

I wasn't smiling, though, when the truck arrived and it became apparent someone had to dive down to help hook the car to the pontoon arrangement, then wait around—wet!—till the truck dragged it ever so slowly to the shore and up over the rocks onto dry ground.

"Paint's okay," Jed mused when the car was at last settled on dry land. "How many more scenes do we have with it?"

"Interiors?"

"We can do those in studio in a mock-up." He paced as he considered. I'd seen him go at it for half an hour, driving other guys as high-strung as he was crazy.

"Exteriors? Distant shots, not a problem"—I was thinking, too. "So we're talking close exteriors. How many? How many essentials?"

"If we—"

"Where d'you want me to take this piece of crap?" The tow driver motioned to our junker.

Jed strode toward it, turned back toward us. "I need to look at the storyboard again. Got to check with—"

"Hey! I have to get this thing out of here. So where you want me to take it?"

"I don't know if we absolutely have to have it at all. Maybe—"

"You're not leaving it here." The cop had a one-track mind.

It was going to take longer to arrange, and—dammit—going to involve me longer, but there was no other alternative. "Let's haul it back to the garage where it was in the city and let it dry out while we decide."

"San Fran? Shit, I can't drag this over the bridge. I'm going to have to get a trailer for that."

"Yeah, sure. Do it." To me Jed said, "You can handle this?" He looked toward the cameras, lights, all the equipment brought over here, unused, needing to be schlepped back to the city. Naturally, he was calculating how much this wasted day cut into our budget.

"Yeah, I'll deal with the car. You going to go to the hospital and check on Mac?"

"Hospital! Yeah, I suppose. One more pain-in-the-ass problem the . . . pain-in-the-ass's adding to this pain-in-the-ass of a day. If he'd planned it he couldn't have screwed things up more."

"Do you think he did?"

"Planned it? Anything's possible, with him."

Not the tack you took when you were hot for me to give him driving lessons. But it wasn't the time to go into that. Particularly when I had much worse to put on the table. "On the drive here he said he had money problems. He sounded like his deal with the Adamés is falling through."

"Shit! *Shit!* Oh shit!" Jed glared at me. "Why didn't you let the bastard drown? We've got insurance. He's dead, he's golden."

Did Mac know that? Was that what he was doing? His own "one decent thing"? Or, like he said, was it all about feeling used?

"Did he clue in Harmon?"

The real producer? "Doubt it. Sounded like he was blurting it out for the first time."

"Shit!" he repeated. "Yeah, okay, I gotta call Harmon. He can go over to the hospital with me. He can sort out this mess."

I nabbed some dry clothes from costumes—a halter top and cargo pants—caught Jed before he headed off, and guilted him out of his black jacket. "I have to get some soup before I deal with the car. You want to come?" But he only scowled, not even bothering to answer.

I stopped to buy the thickest T-shirt in the tackle shop—BERZERKELY MARINA it said under a drawing of a boat with hippies on the deck and protest signs for sails. I wondered how many decades they'd been praying for some tourist to take it off their hands. I inside-outed it and hoped the colors would run in the wash.

After that, I downed a bowl of clam chowder. Shane, the tow driver, was waiting for me.

"You know that tow lot on Folsom—the wrecking yard?"

"Granger's? Yeah, we got an arrangement with them. You want to—"

"Our garage is a couple blocks from there."

He shrugged. As I climbed into the cab he said what I'd already learned: "Most people have no idea how shallow the bay is."

It was a lousy, stupid ending for Mac. Maybe if I'd known him before I would have suspected he was flipping out these last couple days when he plopped into the car on the set and refused to leave, when he offered me a fortune that he knew he didn't have—sheesh!

But now, as I leaned back against the padded seat in the warm tow truck cab, with the faded tobacco smell and Elvis strumming through the speakers and the San Francisco skyline growing larger as we crossed the bridge, there was nothing separating me from a long hot bath and a very big meal other than getting home. Well, except for opening the garage and guiding Shane as he lowered the sodden old Civic into it. So I could toy with compassion. Now, instead of Macomber Dale, the annoying threat to my employment, and Jed's and my relationship with the city film commission, the threat to my whole future, I dipped my toe in the picture of a man losing not only his money but his self-image. A guy facing humiliation, helplessness, ridicule. A man sufficiently unhinged to lock onto the only escape he could find—to drown himself in the bay.

The problem was, I wasn't through with being pissed off. I looked out the windshield at the streets of the outer Mission and felt myself at one with universal grumpiness. You couldn't get more cranky than I felt. But this strange contract with Varine, I needed to get to the bottom of that. Despite his many infuriating qualities, Dale did not seem threatening, dangerous, hardly worth killing yourself for.

Then again, a couple hours ago I wouldn't have been able to imagine him undermining the movie or driving into the bay.

"*This* is it?" Shane stopped across the street from the ramshackle garage. "I thought there was money in filmmaking."

There's nothing like seeing something through the eyes of a stranger to make you realize how well you'd been deluding yourself.

"Yeah, well, my dad got a deal on it years ago and every so often it comes in handy. Like now."

He was staring. "Even this, you could sell it. I mean, property in San Francisco . . ."

"Shane, I've got six brothers and sisters, and a mother. Making a decision about anything at all, ever, is a miracle. Trust me, it's not worth the effort."

I opened the door, jumped down to the sidewalk, and walked across the street, pausing only momentarily to let a truck by. Next to our garage on one side was an auto repair shop—closed and dark. The stucco block on the other side—a mate in decrepitude to ours—hadn't been occupied in ages. If my brother Gary didn't need to park one of his extra cars here, I could leave the junker to rot through eternity.

I jiggled the lock, the doors fell open, and I motioned to Shane. I had the feeling he wanted me to turn on the light, but we hadn't paid for electricity here for, well, ever. As I watched him backing up the truck, I realized that the garage's main function in our family was as a talisman to my father's memory.

The taillights outlined the piles of dried-up paint cans and cardboard boxes.

"Wait a minute!" I didn't remember the stuff being so far into the room. If I shoved—

"Omigod! *Omigod! No!*"

I BENT DOWN over the body, squinting against the dim light and deep shadows in the back of the garage. Time slowed like cells in a reel of film. I saw a person lying face down in the pile of rags. A woman in a latte-brown suit. Just a woman—it didn't have to be her. Her knees were bent, her shins covered in black boots with brown trim. The clothes Marc, the bellman, had described—anyone could have walked through the hotel lobby, spotted them, bought them. It didn't have to be her.

Her hair was chin-length, dark, and matted to the back of her head. Matted with blood!

The *back* of her head. She'd been struck. Killed. She hadn't killed herself—someone had beat her to it!

She was cold. Like she'd been on the bridge. No, not like that at all. She was cold now because she'd been dead for hours. I looked at her face. Blood had pooled on the side nearest me.

Someone had killed her! Picked her up, laid her in a vehicle, and driven her . . . here! I couldn't be sure—that was the cop's job—but that's what it looked like.

But why? Who knew about our garage? Only Mike had any inkling about this woman.

The grind of the tow truck reverberated off the walls, bringing me out of my reverie.

I made it only to the side of the building before I threw up.

Shane gave me water. I washed out my mouth. The air was still but I could feel it on the wetness around my mouth. I stood there numbly. Just stood. It was a couple minutes before I could make myself go back into the garage and double-check what I couldn't believe I had seen.

I scanned the area around her for a purse—none. No purse, no pouch. I wanted to leave it at that, but made myself feel her pockets—no cash, not even a tissue. But in her breast pocket was a credit card: Varine Adamé.

I wanted to stay with her, for no sensible reason, just to do it. But I had to get outside in the air.

Shane, the tow truck driver, was pulling out his cell to call 911. Once he'd done that he started grumbling about his truck and the junker still on the carrier, all the while standing with his back to the garage, as if rejecting the reality of what lay beyond. Finally, I told him to slide the car down next to the curb. I was as relieved as he was to have something do.

But there wasn't any space at the curb and he ended up leaving it on the sidewalk just clear of the garage doors. It sat right next to the space between the garage and the next building, right next to where I'd thrown up.

When the police squealed into view, lights flashing, sirens keening, figures racing around, it all seemed overblown and irrelevant.

"Do you know the deceased?" the detective asked.

"I don't know."

She heaved a big heavy, theatrical sigh. She'd told me her name but it had floated by me. She was young, African American, brusque.

From the doorway, I could see into the garage, to the body lying on her side in that vintage brown suit. I thought I could make out a wrinkle around the hips from the skirt riding up as she pedaled, but I might have been imagining. She looked so "tossed away." Like the rags Gary, Mike, or Gracie'd used to clean windshields when they'd had cars here, the rags John ranted about, not because he cared about them but because they might be a fire hazard and endanger some other discarded belongings.

I didn't save you from jumping for this! I felt like screaming at the stupidity of it all. The waste. *What is life?* I had hunted down, considered, imagined so much of a life for her. Ironically, without ever knowing her, I already missed her. And I would go on missing her, because . . . I didn't know her.

If only I had met her.

Suddenly, I realized that on some level, I'd been assuming that would happen, that we'd sit over coffee and she'd tell me what had moved her to climb over that railing. She'd tell me what she'd been thinking as she biked out there in the cold fog. Having been ready to die, she'd tell me what life is.

She'd say she was glad that I understood.

If only I hadn't wasted my day driving to Berkeley, getting caught up in Mac's whatever the hell it was. His dumb leap into the too shallow water, his non-life-threatening injury.

Could all that have simply been a diversion?

If only I'd hunted her down, found her before . . . what?

Before she died this way! *Devastated* is one of those words so overused that the meaning's almost wrung out of it. But that barren emptiness in which nothing will grow again, that's how I felt. I could have bawled.

But not in front of the police.

Before I walk to the start mark for any gag, before I run through it in my mind the final time, before I even push up into the skin of the character, I exhale, empty my mind, and stare at whatever's ahead as if none of the objects have names, as if there is no space between them and me. I did that now, staring at the tow truck's fender, at the shining in the light, against the shadows, at the curve above the wheel.

Then I turned to the detective. "Yes, I've seen her."

"Her name?"

"Doesn't she have any ID?"

She nodded. "What is it you've seen?"

I started giving her the background but everything I said sounded ludicrous and there was, frankly, little chance this apparently logical woman believed a bit of it.

"And now," she said, "this body's in your garage."

"How'd you know—? Oh, Shane. Okay. Yes, my family owns it. I'm renting the place to the movie company."

"To house this car that you drive."

"In the movie."

"Just that? You never drive it otherwise?"

How'd she know that? Or was she fishing? "Not much."

"But you've done so? Come to this garage to pick up the car and return it."

"I have, but not today. Not alone. The whole film crew knows where this is. Everyone knows the lock's useless. Macomber Dale came here this morning!" *Macomber Dale!* "I've been dropped here by Aaron Adamé and—and!—Declan Serrano! This garage might as well be in Union Square. I spent hours with the Berkeley Police, on the pier over there. I haven't been alone all day, believe me."

"I'm not asking that."

"Uh huh? Then what are you asking me?"

She eyed her notepad, but I had the feeling that was just to buy time, to try to get a linear sense of this tangle.

"Here," I said, "let me take a shot at what you should be asking: How come a woman tries to kill herself, then ends up with someone smashing her head in and dumping her body in a stranger's garage? Why didn't she take her new chance at life and get out of the city?" I turned away. I was on the thin edge of losing it. But I could see the way this investigation was going, and one thing I knew was I didn't have the luxury of falling apart.

"Call Aaron Adamé, her husband," I told her. "She came home last night, or, at least, that's what he told me."

"We can deal with that. The question now is: Why is her body *here*, in *your* garage?"

That *was* the question. "If you drove by here alone, you'd think: good place to hide something. No one's going to be coming here."

"No one but you."

"But *I* wasn't here this morning. I'd driven that"—I jabbed a finger at the miserable remains of the car—"to my place last night. It's a fluke I'm here now. That car was in the bay. We had to drag it out. By rights it should still be under ten feet of water. It's only because we managed to haul it out and then had to put it somewhere that I came back here at all."

She was staring oddly at me. "You drove the car into the bay?"

"No, not me. Macomber Dale. It was an accident. Maybe. He was upset. I don't know why he did it, but he did."

"Where is this Dale?"

"In the hospital. Highland? Herrick? Somewhere near Berkeley." Macomber Dale? "He came here this morning to pick up the car, but the car wasn't here, because I'd taken it home last night."

"Wait here." She strode into the garage.

I weighed my options. I didn't have options. I waited. I watched her check with a uniformed officer, mutter, "Not home? The husband?" A tech handed her something.

While she was inside, a crime scene van pulled up and another patrol car. Doors opened and slammed. Flashers fought with flashers turning the street red, redder, then sucking out all color and leaving it gray as death. A woman hauled out the lighting; a guy grabbed a bag that could have held anything.

An unmarked pulled up. The head that popped out of it was tan, bald, and all too familiar. Declan Serrano.

He had no business here.

I eased back into the shadow.

The cockroach's engine was racing. Or, rather, it sounded that way against the sudden silence. No one was bantering. The techs headed into the garage where the smell was strong enough to drive me out. They looked eager to get in. And the detective who'd been questioning me looked suddenly stiff.

What I needed was to get out of here before Serrano zeroed in on me. Of course, he knew I was here. Of course, he already knew this was my garage. He'd know that and what this detective knew plus a whole lot more. I wanted to bolt.

But he'd hired the woman known as Tessa Jurovik to run his copy service. If he hadn't cared about her as a person, he'd at least been concerned about her as a part of his kingdom.

He strode through the garage to her body. The techs all but leapt back. He stood, looking down as one of the techs starting talking fixed rigor and pointing to her arms.

Serrano dismissed him with a nod. He moved so he was nearly leaning against the wall, staring down at her face, not the way the techs had, but rather as if he was fitting this piece of evidence, her being dead, into a jigsaw in his head. Abruptly he turned away.

The techs watched him go. They, and the cops, looked like they were holding their breaths.

"Hey!" I called out. "What do you make of this?"

"Not my business."

"Hardly! She worked for—"

He shot a hand up, then opened the passenger door of his car.

His phone rang. He ignored it.

I slid in. Before I had the door shut he'd started the car, pulled away from the curb, and swung left around the corner.

His phone rang again. Again, he let it go onto the message but put it onto speaker. It surprised me that my listening wouldn't bother him. Was he that innocent? Or that cocky?

"*Detective*," a woman said, emphasizing the first syllable in a way I'd never heard before, "the missing person's report was filed at nine this morning. Mr. Adamé said he hadn't filed earlier because he *be*lieved he had to wait three days. He stated he'd *be*lieved his wife employed an alias but that now he *be*lieves she's not using that anymore. He stated that he now *be*lieves she's missing. Copy on your desk. No *re*sponse from subject since. Not on landline; not on cell. No one at the residence."

The woman's delivery was so idiosyncratic I wondered how Serrano ever focused on her content. Aaron Adamé had made a missing person's report at nine this morning! But had never bothered to call me back? What did that mean?

"So, Roach, the Adamés played you."

His jaw tightened so slightly I would've missed it if I hadn't been on the lookout. He knew what I meant. But he was waiting for me to spell out just what I knew.

I was happy to do so. "You spotted a woman who you assumed was a ringer for the wife of the guy you're after. Did you have a plan for her? Or did you—ah, yes, I can see this is it—you figured she was too good to pass up. There'd be some way you could use her. So you set her up in a marginal business, like a dog you feed just enough so it doesn't starve but doesn't have the energy to run off—"

"Hey! She was doing okay. She turned that business—"

I laughed. *Good for her!* "But you didn't guess that Adamé had planted Varine for you to find. He put her there to keep an eye on you. Maybe more. Ah, Roach, he was playing your game, only better. When this gets out the whole Mission district'll be laughing. Full rigor," I said without pause for the big change of subject. "So that'd mean she was killed before midnight?"

"Maybe." He shrugged.

"The coroner—"

"Won't say more." *Before midnight.* I'd been with him for dinner, with Adamé after that, which left either one of them plenty of free time. And Macomber Dale, the guy who admitted being at the mouse hole this morning, had been out of my sight almost all night.

"What'd they ask you?" Serrano demanded.

It took me a moment to realize "they" was the detective. "About the garage. Who knew about it."

"You said?"

You. I said, "Macomber Dale, the crew, Adamé. Why?"

"What else?"

"Who she was. I told them to call Adamé."

"You told them that?"

"Hey, I'm a law-abiding citizen."

He shook his head. Then he pulled to the curb. "You know you could've been stuck in the station all night. I saved you. You should be thanking me." He reached across me and shoved open the door.

216

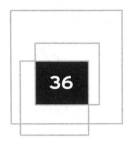

36

SERRANO PULLED AWAY, leaving me on a garbage-strewn corner convenient to nothing. He made another right and headed south. He was going
somewhere fast, and I needed to know where. And, more to the point, why.

But it didn't matter where, because I had no wheels.

And even if I had them, he'd be out of sight before I could tail him.

But, dammit, he didn't light out of here like that for nothing. He may
not have known what I did, but I sure didn't have a clue what he was after.

I had to get a car and I had to delay him. Long shots both. The car
would take some doing, but if I didn't slow up Serrano first, the car wouldn't
matter.

And when he realized I'd set him up, he'd be out for bear.

I slipped into the first alley. If Serrano noted my phone number on his
cell phone I'd be . . . bear. But he hadn't paid attention before. If he answered—but he hadn't always done that either. I spent precious seconds
picturing myself at a desk outside his office. Then I punched in his number.

"Leave a message."

I was so relieved I almost sighed. "*Detective,* the chief's on his way to
the crime scene. He's *de*manding to talk to you. He's—" I garbled a couple
words and hung up. Then I pulled out the tow company card and called
Shane. "Are you still at the garage?"

"Yeah, I'm here. Cooling my heels watching nothing. Car's sitting at the curb where I left it. No point in me being here. I got nothing to say. I told them, the lot of 'em. I got—"

"Okay, okay, I get the idea! The tow lot on Folsom, you said you've got an arrangement with them. Can I pick up a car there?"

"Hey, those cars belong to people. They're not Avis." Suddenly he was all business. "I've got standards, principles—"

"How much?"

"Five for the night."

"Two and I need to be out the gate in five minutes."

"Hey, I can't even get outta here in that time."

"Make a call. Extra hundred."

"Okay, but I'm not promising condition. Like I said, it's only an arrangement, me with them, not like I—. And you gotta have it back by morning."

I double-checked the address and ran.

By the time I hit the tow yard I was panting too hard to speak. The car, a Camaro, was a CHP magnet, and white, the easiest color to spot on the road. "Why'd . . . this get towed?"

His reply was a take-it-or-leave-it shrug. I took the keys.

The surest spot to pick up Serrano'd be the one place I didn't dare show my face—the crime scene. But I had an advantage there. After all the years of dropping off cars at the mouse hole, waiting for my brothers or my sister, Gracie, after they'd parked in the garage, I knew the area. The first year I had my license, I'd followed John, waited while he picked up something, tailed him home without being made, and won five bucks each from my other brothers.

The alley I'd used back then was on the far side of the cross street. Serrano'd have to pass me when he left.

I circled around, got caught at two red lights, and had barely turned into the alley when my phone rang.

"Mike! I'm a little busy. What's up?"

Brakes screeched. The crime scene! Serrano! He slammed out of the car, grabbed the nearest guy in blue. He was yelling. Running, banging back into the car. Tires squealed as he shot forward, did a 180, and flew past my corner.

I hit the gas.

"What's going on?"

"I'm on his tail."

"Whose tail?"

"Cockroach. Gotta go." I tossed the phone on the seat.

Serrano was three blocks ahead and moving out. If he made the light at Cesar Chavez he'd be on the freeway before I finished looking at red. He'd be heading south, or north, and I'd have no idea which.

I stepped on it, closing in. Just a block between us.

The light at Cesar Chavez turned amber. Serrano shot through and swung left.

I cleared it as amber turned to red, barely missing a van when it jumped the light.

All three lanes of Cesar Chavez—formerly Army Street—were jammed and moving fast. I cut right, in front of a truck. Now an SUV with dark windows clogged the view. I veered right again. Was he in this center lane? That'd mean he was headed under the underpass, aiming to go downtown.

No sign of him.

I moved left. A horn blared behind me. Two cars ahead was Serrano, easing onto the on-ramp. He was getting on the freeway south. I followed close; I had bigger worries than being spotted.

I grabbed the phone and called Mike. "He's going south—south!—on 101! Maybe he'll head for the coast, but—"

"Yeah, odds are the airport."

"'xactly. Any chance you can see reservations?"

"You want me to hack into airline reservations? You must think I'm God."

"Are you?"

"Maybe."

"Can you check for Serrano?"

"Not if he just bought a ticket. Nothing gets posted that fast."

I nodded as if to say okay, as if he could see me. "If he's headed to SFO, he's after Aaron Adamé—"

"Because?"

"Serrano doesn't care about the murder. He's after Adamé. Adamé's kept him at bay for years. By now it's personal. He thought he was setting up a sting of sorts with a double for Adamé's wife, but instead, Adamé stung him. And I just stung him again. He's pissed. He's not wasting time."

"So where're you getting all this?"

"Mike, the cops have a murdered woman. Her body's lying in the mouse hole. Adamé made a missing person's report this morning and now he's not answering his cell. A worried husband would be glued to it. The twenty years you were missing, Mike, Mom never left the house more than an hour."

He paused just an instant before saying, "Gotcha."

"Can you find Tessa—or Varine—whichever name—"

"The dead woman? She's not likely to be flying."

"I know that! But they didn't, not before today."

"Hey, this is tricky stuff you're asking. Maybe I can get a look, but it's not like there's a central index for all flights out of SFO. It'll be glance and split and that's if I can work it at all. So, which one do you want?"

Which one? "Tessa."

"Okay? And?"

"Was there a reservation for her? When's it for? How long ago was it made? Who made it? But you probably can't—"

"Not that, no. Why do you care about when?"

"Was it before or after the bridge?"

"Are you thinking—"

"Maybe."

"O . . . kay. See what I can do for ya." He clicked off.

Ahead, Serrano was driving like a guy who wasn't worried about tickets. I was doing eighty just keeping him in sight. He swished passed the 280 turnoff for the beaches, and the coast road. So, unless he knew the way to San Jose, he was headed to the airport.

He pulled into the fast lane. Okay for him, but too dangerous for me in a white sporty car. I sidled into the number two.

There's a reason the fast lane's called the fast lane. I was losing him. I shot in behind him, two cars back, hung there a couple minutes, swung back into number two.

I was losing him again. I had to chance the fast lane. I shot a glance in the rearview. Damn! The Highway Patrol was keeping pace. I just had room to cut in and back out.

I eased only my head to the left, trying to keep my target in sight. The CHP car slowed behind him. For a minute I thought Serrano was going to get pulled over.

I slid in behind and matched the patrol car's speed.

My phone rang.

Speeding behind the CHP, talking on the phone! Was I insane?

"Tessa Jurovik, flight to Miami on Delta. Layover in Atlanta. Sunday morning."

"The day we were on the bridge." My breath caught.

"But no flight, just a reservation."

"What do you mean?"

"Flight got canceled."

"Canceled?" I could barely breathe at all. "You mean, she backed away?"

"No, the airline canceled. Remember that fire on the runway in Atlanta?"

"No. Why would I? Why would that make news here?"

"Yeah, well, never mind. Here's the good news. She rescheduled to Raleigh-Durham and flew out last night."

"She went? She flew out?" I gasped and had to gasp again before I could breathe. "Mike, do you realize what that means? She's alive! She's okay. She's not lying dead in the mouse hole! She's . . . oh."

He didn't say anything. I remembered that fine quality of his—not saying anything stupid when there was nothing to say.

"Oh," I repeated. "Right. Someone's still lying there dead."

"But you recognized her? How?"

"Her clothes, her hair. But—wait!—Serrano didn't care about that. He checked her face. Mike, he knows them both."

"So, why's he making for the airport?"

"That's what I intend to find out."

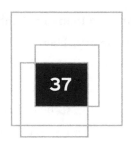

I SNAGGED HIM at the security check.

The whole population of the city and county of San Francisco had queued up there. But Declan Serrano wasn't the type to be standing in line. He'd cut through to the front, ready to flash his shield and stride through.

"Hey, Serrano! Wait!"

His shield and boarding pass were on the portable counter, his hand atop both. The airport security woman was on the phone. The drive here'd been so frantic I'd had no time to organize questions. I blurted out, "Who is she?"

Serrano did not even turn around.

The security woman proffered his boarding pass. "You're cleared through, Detective."

I grabbed his arm and pulled him back to face me. "Varine or Tessa?"

He shook off my hand, picked up the paper, and strolled through to the gate.

The security woman glared at me and picked up her phone.

I smiled. He was what he was. I hadn't really expected any help. But while I'd had his arm I'd noted his boarding pass. His flight was Southwest to Raleigh-Durham!

Southwest Airlines had more than one flight to Raleigh-Durham. I got standby for the last flight of the day. There's no overdraft protection on the luck account, and this was a huge withdrawal.

I raced back to a check-in machine, punched in my six-figure code, and in twenty minutes was back in the security line, sadly at the other end. I did what everyone else did, dialed my phone. First, I got a rental car out of Raleigh. Then I called the long distance number Tessa—Tessa? Varine?— had called from the Presidential Suite.

No answer.

Tessa! I'd been so happy she was real. I hadn't even bothered to consider how ridiculous that was. I'd just been glad, like a friend had come back. Like Mike, after all those years he was gone and people'd told us to "move on." But he'd come back. And it was wonderful.

Hope is an illusion. I know that. But it's the hardest one to give up.

I pulled up the internet and tried the reverse directory. Not listed.

Tessa or Varine? A long distance call didn't signal one or the other.

I checked the area code. North Carolina. East of Raleigh.

Why would Tessa call there? How could I find out?

How? I was holding my breath, willing Tessa to have flown east, to be alive!

How?

I called Kristi. "Hi! Darcy Lott here. Quick question. Remember Tessa's lout of a boyfriend?"

"Well, ye-ah!"

"Was he in North Carolina?"

"I dunno."

"But he called?"

"Well, ye-ah. She just about flew to the phone when it rang."

"Did she tell you—"

"You want the number?"

"What number?"

"The one the lout called from."

"From North Carolina?"

"Wherever!"

I poised my pen. "Shoot."

The same number! The one she called from the Mark Hopkins! The woman in the Presidential Suite called Tessa's boyfriend in North Carolina! She was Tessa!

I had to swallow hard to even speak. "How come you have it?"

"I took the message, well, the call-back number for Tessa a couple weeks ago."

"Weeks ago? But you didn't throw away your copy of the number?"

"Why would I? I mean, you never know when something like that's going to be useful. Like now, right? I kept the copy, you know, from the message pad. You're glad I did, aren't you? Right?"

"I am, truly, yes. But listen, how is it you had that number at your fingertips just now?"

"Like I said, I stuck it in my wallet. I fished it out for the boss. He called half an hour ago."

The boss—Serrano. "About North Carolina—the boyfriend's number?"

"Well, yeah. But, like, when he called, I was having a drink and the place was really loud and I could barely make out his question and, well, you know, it wasn't the place to go pulling stuff out of your wallet."

"He gave you a call-back number, right?"

"Sure. And I actually did call him—it wasn't easy either. I mean, I had to go outside onto Valencia and try to find a quiet spot, and you know that's no small deal, and then when I call, the guy doesn't bother answering. So, I think, screw him, right?"

"You got his voicemail?"

"Yeah."

"Did you leave any message? Give him the Carolina number?" I was holding my breath.

"Hell no. He's so hot to have it and then he can't—"

Whew! "Kristi! Listen, I know him; I've got his number, I'll deal with this. You've done your part. Tessa'll be grateful."

"Okay, sure."

"Wait! Quick question. That boyfriend. Did Tessa actually say he was her boyfriend?"

"Her? No way. Too personal. I understood. I mean, bad enough to be the victim without having to talk about it, you know? I could've told her— but we both acted like those calls never happened, you know?"

"Yeah." I did know.

"Listen, I'm at the airport. I'll be in touch when I get back. We'll go out, have a drink with Tessa, okay?"

"Tessa, she's okay? I mean, you saved her. She's okay now, right?"

I started to say yes! But the word stuck in my throat and I found myself speaking a truth I hadn't realized. "I hope so."

"But—"

"I'm at the security gate. Gotta go." I hesitated. "I'll call you."

I yanked off my shoes, plunked my pack in the basket, and barefooted it through the gate.

The guard pulled me aside.

But I was so happy about Tessa, so relieved she wasn't lying dead in the mouse hole, that I just smiled and trotted after her to be scanned more closely.

Grudgingly, she passed me.

It wasn't till I caught sight of myself in the window of one of the shops that I understood what happened. Me, in my inside-out BERZERKELY T-shirt and scabrous pants. My hair didn't look so hot either. I looked like a terrorist from an impoverished and tasteless nation. I'd have to deal with that . . . later.

I checked the departures board for my flight and got a surprise. Declan Serrano's flight hadn't taken off. Delayed! Rarely does that word produce a grin, but it sure did now.

"Hey," I called out across the crowd when I made it to his gate. He was standing near the counter, phone out.

Chats are much more promising when you've got something the other guy wants and your biggest problem is deciding what you'll take for it. "Whatever that conversation is," I said in a low pleasant voice, "it's not as important as the one you're about to have with me."

He didn't jump out of his skin, but he gave a rewarding little jolt backward and clicked off the phone without even a "later." "What? Where'd you come from? Did you get on this flight?"

I smiled. Which was more satisfying than saying no. "I had some spare time in line back there, so I called Kristi. She's considered your request, remembered what she's heard."

"And?"

"You first. How come you—"

"You withholding evidence?"

"Not on any case you're involved with. That crime scene, I don't recall you being in charge."

He stepped in closer.

I held my ground. "Declan, we're in a very public place."

"I'm not fooling around here."

"Nor I. I'll tell you what I know. But only after you listen to what I want. Buy or pass."

We are going to start preboarding for families with small children . . .

"This is between us," he said, lowering his voice.

"First," I said, "I'm on standby on the next flight. Get me on it."

"What? If I could manage—"

"Time passes."

I watched him pull out his shield, lean cozily over the counter, and smile. It might have meant anything, but I had no fall-back position, so I opted for picturing the best case.

"Number one, standby, on the flight you're booked on. Now you."

"How'd you know about the phone number in North Carolina?"

"Where'd you—"

"I ask. You answer." *As the cops say.*

"I'm not fooling around here."

I shrugged. I was enjoying this.

"I have my sources."

Kristi? Did I misjudge her that much? "Which are? Come on, we're not in the station now! How'd you know about it?"

"Background checks. It's what detectives do. Have sources they check out. Now give!"

"I thought you didn't background Tessa."

"I didn't. Now give!"

"Tessa called him from the Mark Hopkins, the night before she tried to kill herself."

He nodded.

"You knew that?"

"What?"

"That this is the same guy she was calling from the copy shop?"

"Yeah."

"I don't believe you."

He shrugged just as I had. "The number?"

I gave it to him. "Wait for me in Raleigh."

The cockroach laughed.

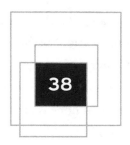

38

IF SERRANO DIDN'T background Tessa—no reason for him to lie about that—why did he care about her boyfr—

Oh shit! The roach didn't background *her*. The guy on the phone *wasn't* her boyfriend. So, then, who was he? I needed to buy a winter jacket and some not-scuzzy clothes before I got on a plane, but, once again, that'd have to wait. I called Mike.

My call went to voicemail.

In five minutes I had new black pants, sweater, and jacket and was ordering one of those burgers that have more calories than the average gorilla's daily intake, and a latte—a single, so I could sleep on the plane—and redialed. "You were talking to someone else?"

"Hey, you turned off your phone!"

That was another thing we'd never done to each other. "Sorry. But the cockroach—he's headed to Raleigh."

"After Adamé." It wasn't even a question, and hearing it aloud from Mike confirmed all my fears.

"Mike, Serrano didn't have the number . . . till I gave it to him." My food arrived, but now I didn't feel much like eating.

"Oh. And now he can get the address," Mike said in a resigned tone that echoed my own.

"Maybe. But, listen, Tessa's *got* to be all right!"

He let a beat pass before he said, "Because you want her to be?"

Wanting something doesn't make it so. I had to get a grip. I needed time to sit zazen, to step back from the desperation of my thoughts, to see life as it is. To remind myself that hope is an illusion. But here I was in the airport with a table full of food I couldn't face and a latte. All I could do was take a deep breath and try to not "look through my own eyes," as my old teacher in New York had told me years ago. I tried to see objectively. I took a sip of the coffee. "Two women," I said. "Sunday, one of them would have flown to Miami, the other would've jumped off the bridge. That was the plan. The *contract*. But the flight got canceled."

"And you pulled the other woman back."

"The woman on the bridge—my woman—which one is she? She'd used Varine Adamé's credit card. The woman on the plane carried Tessa Jurovik's ID . . . ?"

"Yeah . . . "

"Okay, so one thing's clear: Tessa Jurovik is *not* an alias for Varine," I said just to hear it out loud. "Tessa is not an alternate life Varine created. There were two women, who looked a lot alike."

"Enough to pass for each other to people who didn't know them?"

"Right. I saw a picture of Varine in the Adamés' house."

"You sure it was her? That Adamé didn't have Tessa pose?"

That threw me for a moment. "No, it was a picture of his wife, on display in his house. Adamé didn't know I was coming. I just arrived at his door. He wasn't out of my sight the whole time I was there."

"Makes sense. Anything else'd be a big stretch. But, Darce, I've been thinking about this. You said Tessa's been arrested for shoplifting, so if she lifted Varine Adamé's ID—"

"Cockroach! That came from Serrano! One of his probably fishy tales of how he met her."

"But—"

I lifted my cup, then put it down. "Wait, we've got this backward, thinking Tessa took Varine's ID. But Varine using Tessa's ID, that's a whole different world."

"How so?" Mike's words were suddenly sharper, faster, *into-it* in a way I hadn't heard since he'd come home. I could almost see him leaning forward. "Start with the woman on the bridge. Who was she?"

"Tessa, wearing Varine's jacket. So, the camera on the bridge saw 'Varine Adamé' try to jump. If Adamé said his wife was depressed—which he did—and missing—which he did—no one would question it. Even acquaintances, people she only met at affairs like the City Hall deal, knew she loathed the life she had."

"And the Mark Hopkins?"

"Again, Tessa using Varine's ID! For a last fling before she had to go to the bridge and jump."

"Fling? From what you've said about Tessa, she's not the fling type."

"Point taken."

"But someone—"

"Right! Mike, Tessa was still doubling as Varine at that point. So she was showing the world Varine Adamé spending a night apart from her husband, in the Presidential Suite, an escapade bound to raise eyebrows when it came out."

"Hot night with the bellman? All the better, eh?"

"Those desperate phone calls Tessa made the day before, phone calls to her boyf—No, wait, the guy on the phone knew she was going to the Presidential Suite. That was the plan. She wasn't calling a lover, she was trying to get out of jumping! That's why she was calling! Oh, God, poor Tessa! Then on the bridge you drove up, you beeped, she hoped that at that last moment he'd changed his mind. That she wouldn't have to die after all."

Mike was silent, too. I just sat, wrung out from losing Tessa, then getting her back. Maybe. I so desperately wanted her to be alive and safe.

But she wasn't, not safe, not relieved, maybe not even alive. Had I saved her just so she could be bludgeoned and dumped in a ratty garage? I felt so awful, so empty, so angry, so miserable that all I could do was go stiff against the emotion and narrow my focus to what Mike was saying.

"Look, I've been in tight spots these last years. I've made deals with the devil. If you knew about them you'd wonder if I was the kid you grew up with. But jumping off the Golden Gate, that's so far out it's . . . it's just wacko. Tessa had to have a huge carrot or an enormous stick to make her do something as extreme as that. She made some deal. After you saved her, are you saying that deal was voided when the airline canceled Varine's flight Sunday? How could that—"

"I don't know. Things change. That's what I'm saying: Things change."

Announcements came over the PA system. I'd been ignoring them. I looked toward my gate. People were grabbing their coats and carry-ons and wedging themselves into line. I walked toward the gate.

I swallowed hard. "I'm pretty sure why she did it, but my flight's starting to board. Right now I need to think about the other side—Varine. Why have it appear that Varine Adamé killed herself?"

"To cover her getaway," he said as if it was too obvious to put into words. "So, what's she escaping from?"

What *was* Varine Adamé running away from? That was a no-brainer. "The cockroach, who else?" I couldn't keep from saying it in exactly the same tone. But now I was talking to myself as much as him. "Serrano's after Adamé big time. So, Varine books a flight to Miami, gateway to points Caribbean. It gets canceled. Then why didn't she reschedule for Miami?"

"Because she's dead." Had he said that or had I? I went on, "Why did Tessa Jurovik fly to Raleigh last night? Why is Adamé flying to Raleigh? Did his wife—"

"—find out?" my brother mused. "And Adamé has to murder her to cover his own escape?"

"The line's moving, Mike. I've got to pay attention; I'm on standby. I'll call you."

39

I'm a city girl. I used to have a serious—and seriously humiliating—fear of forests. I'm better now; I can walk under leaves and fronds without going queasy, but dark green overhead blocking out the light is never likely to be a favorite with me. It was going to be dark when I arrived, but that was hardly going to make things better. In the meantime, I employed one of my great talents: I can sleep anywhere. I put my new warm, water-resistant protect-all jacket over my head and didn't come up for air till Nashville. But sometimes sleep isn't just sleep. Not exactly dreams, either. Like meditation, it skims off the surface of flurry and drops you into a great formless pool of common sense. As the plane descended toward Nashville I wondered: Can I just wait and let Serrano go and collect Aaron Adamé? Facing down miscreants and murderers, it's what he does. He's got the phone number, plus a serious lead on me. Why not? See Adamé behind bars? No one hotter was for that than the cockroach. And snag the money Adamé'd made off with? Ditto.

If Adamé and Tessa are in this together and she gets away? Not my problem! Not at all!

But if Tessa got caught in the cross fire? Would Serrano care? Maybe. If saving her meant losing Adamé? Not likely.

What about Tessa? She'd made the deal for Ginger, but once the check cleared and I'd pulled her back, then what? Why didn't she get away? That was the question that I'd always be asking.

Was she even Tessa? I didn't know that. Only Serrano knew.

As I headed for the next gate, I turned on my phone. The message icon danced. I dialed.

"Listen, Darce," Mike said, without letting me speak, "maybe you don't realize what scum the cockroach is."

"I believe I do. I've heard about him for years and—"

"That's family chat. There's stuff John's not saying at dinner."

"I can read between the lines."

"Maybe. But I know Serrano. Know him better than you think. You know that call I got Sunday—"

"The one that was *not* from Mom? Yeah, Mike, I do know."

"I could hardly tell you it was from him, not then, right after the bridge, when you—"

"I know you know him. He told me."

"He told you what?"

Knew your brother when he was running smack. "Not over the phone."

"Listen—"

"That's my boarding call."

"Wait, Darce. Serrano lies. Remember that. Guy lies all the time. But here's the truth, the guy'll do anything—*anything*—for power. Did he give you that righteous rant about how safe he keeps the Mission? You think he cares whether girls can walk home from clubs without being raped? Power and money, that's it! He . . . "

"Seriously, I gotta go!" I clicked off.

The pre-boards rolled and hauled down the chute, and the A pass holders picked up their carry-ons. I was not an A, or a B.

Mike wasn't telling me anything I didn't know, just what he thought I didn't know. And Declan Serrano already had over an hour lead on me.

Still, Mike's call made me nervous and when the phone rang again I checked the number and steeled myself. I barely got out hello when my brother John started in. "Don't you think SFPD is onto Adamé? Why do you think Adamé ran, Darcy, tell me that, will you? We've got an agent in Miami Dade right now. We're working with the department there. We've alerted border control. Do you think SFPD is a nursery school? We've been working this case for close to a year now. We're ready to snap it. Serrano's not on that case. He's rogue. Rogue! Guy figures he sees what no one else does. Thinks he walks a wild side we don't know exists. An egomaniac. Department should've sacked him years ago—"

"Why didn't it, then?"

The pause was so long I thought he'd driven out of range. "Because sometimes he delivers."

"So, tomorrow he could be dragging Adamé into the mayor's office and stepping out of there with a promotion?"

"What I'm saying is you are way, way over your head. You've got no business with him. Where are you?"

"Nashville."

"Turn around. Get on a plane home."

"Fat chance! It was only Serrano pulling strings that got me on this flight."

He sounded like he was choking.

"My plane's boarding. To Raleigh. Serrano's already—"

"I'll have someone meet your flight there. You can brief them. They'll deal with this business. I'll get you a flight home. Call me then."

"What? What? . . . you're breaking up."

"I'm telling you—"

I clicked off. I was fuming, not because of what he'd said, though maybe I should have been, but because Mike had ratted me out to him. We'd had a compact, Mike and I: No matter what, we had never ever ratted out the other.

Was Mike *that* worried? About Serrano?

Or maybe things really had changed between us. Enough, anyway, that when he called back I didn't pick up.

Despite my sleep trick on the next leg, I was still edgy when I walked off the plane in Raleigh.

My first surprise was that there was no local law in sight. No county, state, or feds. There could be a dozen reasons, not the least of which was John was not as well connected as he thought. Or else this case wasn't as high a priority as he thought. Or who knows what?

But I didn't have time to find out, because my second surprise was Serrano, standing there.

"How come you're still here?"

"Don't want you out there driving around in the woods."

"Boy, you've got more concern than a lot of guys I know give you credit for."

He took my arm. "Time passes. Come on."

I shook free. "Not so fast! Biggest danger in the woods could be you."

He laughed.

"I'm not joking. You know about the idiot in the attic?"

"I'm not even going to guess."

"Girl, alone, no weapon but a candle. There's a crazed killer in the neighborhood. She hears a strange sound in the attic. Does she call the police?"

"No?"

"Does she even flee out the front door into the safety of the street? Nope. She lights the candle, climbs the stairs, and opens the attic door. So convince me you're not in the attic."

"I'm going to be straight with you."

"As opposed to?"

He took a deep breath. I couldn't tell if he was merely organizing his thoughts or forming them. "Okay, just between us, right?"

"Lips zipped."

"I don't have a car."

"Excuse me?"

"If I'm on a case, the department handles everything."

I rolled my eyes. "You're going to have to do a lot better than that."

"No, really—"

"Don't even bother."

"I could give you a list of reasons, some of them true. I could get a car but it'd be a hassle."

"And you'd have to do it in your own name."

"Look, Tessa Jurovik's in the woods with a killer. I don't have time to deal with her. You want to be sure she lives, then come."

Bingo! "How can I be sure it's her?"

"It's her," he said resignedly. "She knew what she was getting into. Not when I first hired her, but the instant she saw a picture of Varine Adamé she put it together. Remind me never to hire a woman who reads the society pages."

"She knew you could get her killed?"

"You pulled her back over the railing of the Golden Gate Bridge! She wasn't afraid to live on the edge. She knew I was looking for an angle with Adamé and that she might be it. She was aware of my reputation. I don't sugarcoat that, not with anyone."

"Not called the cockroach for nothing, huh?"

Serrano ignored that. "Okay, here's your deal. Call your brother. Tell him the plan. Let him do whatever he wants. Fair enough?"

Whoa! There had to be a catch, but I couldn't spot it. Except for a small hole which I could circumvent. "Fair enough." I pulled out my phone and called my brother. But I wasn't about to give the cockroach the pleasure of listening to Detective John Lott sputter and threaten over the phone. "Mike, just listen. I'm here with Serrano, at Raleigh-Durham. I've rented a car. The two of us are heading out now, him to collect Adamé, me to do my best to protect Tessa. Tell John. Also tell him that not a single law enforcement employee was visible anywhere when I got off the plane."

"Darce—"

"I'll call you." I clicked off, leaving him hanging. *Again.* I turned to Serrano. "So, what's your plan?"

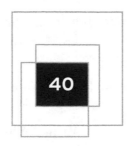

40

I WAS DRIVING. And happy about it. I followed the signs to 40 heading southeast. It's a major highway, but it could've been a two-laner for all the traffic it carried. Maybe Tar Heels didn't do their traveling after midnight.

I glanced over at Serrano. He was shifting restlessly, wedging his feet against the dash. He hesitated, then dropped them back to the floor. "I'll scope the scene and call the locals."

"Yeah, right! If you were going to call in help you'd've done it. So, what's your real plan?"

"Scope the scene, grab Adamé, let *you* call the locals."

"As you sail into the sunset waving good-bye?"

"Sunrise. But you don't have to wait that long." He laughed. "He's a San Francisco felon. I don't want the asshole vacationing in the Raleigh lock-up while his expensive lawyers—paid with money he laundered through my district—throw up every roadblock to extradition."

"Why don't you just shoot him?"

I'd meant it sarcastically. Sort of. "No can do. I already don't have the best reputation. Now if you'd take him out . . . "

"What about Tessa?"

"Tessa?"

"Tessa Jurovik! The woman you dragged into this?" I was trying—failing—to keep calm. "It's the old cockroach problem. You haven't given her a thought, have you?"

"Did you ever stop to think I might be doing her a favor?"

Okay, I thought a minute and got it. Why would Tessa be here if she didn't have some relationship with Adamé? Why hadn't she just headed for the San Francisco city limits and kept on going? Meeting up with him across the country, that showed her in a whole different light. Why—

"If he has some hold over her now, she's free," he said. "If she's not as innocent as you want to believe, well, once he's in the lock-up, she can say whatever she wants. If there's evidence against her, she'll have time to disappear. All good. And, best of all for her, she'll have you there to protect her."

Oh, please!

I looked over at Serrano. He was nodding off. Just as well. I was glad to be "alone." There was only the occasional flash of white to remind me that beyond the dark clumps to my left were westbound lanes. A vehicle passed and then it was darkness again. Our Bay Area freeways are never like that. There are always lights from the cities beside them or at least headlights coming and taillights ahead. There's always the sense of moving toward. But here, I felt like I was alone in a black box.

What is life?

If I were alone in a black box would I still be alive?

Or was the question itself the black box?

As I drove, I felt the resistance of the pedals, tested the give of the steering wheel, felt the tires grab—grab was too strong a word for these tires. I shifted in the seat, noted the push button windows—I don't trust electric releases in emergency. I felt myself in this car the way I did in a stunt car.

What is life? Having come so close to throwing it away, how would Tessa Jurovik answer that now?

I rolled down the window. The air was cold, but the aroma of pine was strong and fresh. I felt my body releasing as I breathed.

In the silence time passed without clocking in. It might have been an hour, or a goodly range on either side when Serrano jerked awake. "How long before the turnoff?" I asked, hardly expecting him to know.

"Twenty minutes."

"Wow. I'm impressed."

"A detective always sleeps with one eye open. That eye's on the road."

I had plenty of questions. Now, with no distractions, it'd be easy for him to sidestep or fabricate entirely. I asked the one he'd be least likely to shirk. "Where's Varine in all this?"

"Varine?" he said so blankly, I wondered if he had slipped back into dreamland. "Ah, the too-bright-to-be-bothered Mrs. Adamé. One of those pain-in-the-ass free spirits. With a husband to float her, she can make a career of having no responsibilities."

"Did she care about Tessa?"

"Doesn't appear so."

"You don't know?" One thing I understood about Serrano was he hated not knowing, or, at least admitting it. But now he just grunted.

I wasn't giving up on this. "You jumped at the chance to hire her double."

"Look, you gotta be open. I wasn't expecting much, but one slip would've made the whole arrangement pop." He shifted to face me. "Adamé said—convinced himself. I believe this, that he convinced himself—that he did his crimes for her. But, see, not really for her, for the *idea* of her."

Someone else'd said that about Adamé. Oh yeah, Warren Llekko, my old classmate, and not the most perceptive of guys. He'd been skeptical. But from Serrano I was getting a different take.

"He made her into an icon—*his* icon—because a guy needs that, he needs someone to trust. Someone who binds it all together. Someone for whom he's number one. It makes all the difference."

"How come you know that?"

"'Cause I never let myself do it."

"How come?" I repeated. The darkness and the car let me ask that dreadfully personal question: How could you get through life without this most basic of comforts? I let the question hang, not expecting an answer.

"Here's the irony," Serrano said after a few moments. "Varine's sharp, sharper than Adamé."

"Not sharp enough to avoid him killing her. How do you see that?"

"Could've been anything from a double cross to a lovers' spat. No difference in the end, though." He peered through the windshield. "Or maybe he was just tired of living with someone who could see through him. He's slick and he hates to lose."

Him or yourself? Something about Adamé'd sure gotten under his skin. Maybe it was just what Serrano'd told me—Adamé invading his turf—or maybe—

I had to swallow hard not to laugh. Dale! "You know what Mac told me? He said the Adamés paid him to hassle you. Could that be—"

"Turnoff's coming up. Third one."

"Mac caused you a ton of problems—woke up the neighbors around our set, called the mayor's office, and that's just what I know about. He pissed you off, distracted you—And, he bought Adamé some time."

And he was laughing at you!

I didn't expect Serrano to comment on that, either, but his silence said it all.

Suddenly, the exits were beside us—all three virtually together—and our ramp was a dark chute into nothingness. The width of the highway had given some illusion of options, but now, as we slowed onto a two lane with trees marching in from both sides, we might as well have been in a tunnel. In a hundred feet the road had narrowed even more to two skinny lanes banked by shrubs that could pass as landmarks only to a local, a cold sober local. I wanted to speed up, but forced myself to slow. Something shot across the road. I just about stood on the brake pedal, but whatever it was was gone. Leaving me ridiculously shaken and aware of how vulnerable I was.

At the first sign of life, a two-pump gas station with a snack shop, I pulled in and hopped out, leaving Serrano in the car.

"We're looking for the Adamés on Hopkins Island and I think we're lost."

The woman, about my age but with a harder history, nodded. Despite the night's chill she was wearing cut-offs and a T-shirt that said CARLENE'S A GAS! "Adamé? That name's not familiar, and I know everyone who owns here. You got an address?"

I handed her the reverse Serrano'd gotten.

She eyed it a moment. "Out on the county road. Those places there, lot of them are abandoned."

"Really? Coastal property? I'd've thought—"

"Too marshy. Not worth the cost. Someday, sure. But now, things as they are, no one goes down that road for anything but to dump trash they're too cheap to run to the incinerator or too lazy to burn."

"I'm amazed. I've been to this area in the spring. When the dogwood's in bloom, there's no prettier place on earth."

She'd been wary but now she gave me a big, knowing smile. "You can say that again, girl."

I liked this woman. I wanted to settle in here and chat behind the safety of the counter. But I bought a couple bottles of water, stuck the change in my coat pocket, along with my phone, just in case, and asked how to get where I was headed.

"This time of night, the quickest way's not the smartest if you don't know our roads. You got to be careful, real careful for a—where you from, girl?"

I considered a lie. Not everyone in the nation thinks of our city as highly as we do. But I'm a third generation San Franciscan. "San Francisco."

"Oh my. My cousin went out there on his honeymoon. He rode one of them cable cars . . . "

I just hoped that was before the fare was six bucks a pop, but if he'd left his fortune in San Francisco he must have kept that to himself. Carleen was smiling.

I repeated her directions. "Straight along this road till it forks in three miles. Right fork. That makes a slow curve. Take it for four miles till I see a road that comes into it at a back angle. That's Sandy Flat Road. I go on that for a mile and a half till I come to their mailbox." *And hope it's got a name or number on it that's big enough to see in the middle of the night.*

I pictured the slow loop to the right she described, leading us to one of those little shingle cottages like there were in the Russian River area under the redwoods. Not likely. "*Right* fork? Isn't that the wrong direction?"

"Guess it does seem that way. Left fork peters out in a mile."

"Okay."

"Good luck, honey. You drive careful, you hear."

"Thanks."

"Directions?" Serrano demanded as I neared the car. He was behind the wheel.

"What're you doing?"

"Time for me to drive."

"Not in my car."

He jiggled the keys. "Possession! You're wasting time. Adamé's not going to wait for sunrise."

I considered arguing for form's sake, but I wanted the chance to observe him. *Serrano lies. Guy lies all the time*, Mike had made a point of telling me. But even for liars the truth is convenient sometimes.

"How far?" he asked, pulling out onto the empty road.

I took a drink of water—it was going to be a long night—and stuck both bottles in the cup holders. "Three miles."

He lies all the time. I knew it, had known it in Nashville, and back at SFO. Still, which things were lies, which not? He knew too much about Adamé, Varine, and Tessa for me to catch him up. I had to shift the game to my field.

"How'd you meet Mike?" I asked.

"Don't remember. It amused me to play him."

My breath caught. "Well, you can stop trying to play me—or is that your entire view of social intercourse?"

"Play or get played?" He paused. "Yeah, guess so."

"Mike?" I insisted. "Did you pick him up—"

"Didn't pick him up at all."

"Then . . . ?"

"Kid walked into my office. Told me he was Lott's brother up front, said he wanted to see the city through the eyes of the cockroach."

"He used that term?" That made me smile: It had to be true.

"Oh yeah. First time I heard it! I was so—maybe that's why I bothered with his challenge."

"What'd he do for you?"

"Undercover. A natural at slipping himself in. Amazing for a guy with as good of looks as you. Great actor. Lousy enforcer."

My every pore sighed with relief. "He wasn't willing to hurt people."

"Nah. Not that. Just that he didn't care. Enforcing's too blunt. No challenge." He turned to me. "By the time he was eighteen he knew my entire operation. Guys on the street trusted him more than me. They confided in him. Come to it, he could've caused me big problems. Big enough that I wrote a friend in Massachusetts who had an in with the senator for a letter to the college for him. I wanted him on the other side of the continent."

I said nothing. It was all I could do to cover my gasp. But I remembered Mike in that easy disguise when I got off the bridge Sunday, and I didn't doubt what I was hearing. "And then?"

"Nothing. Never saw him when he came home from school, if he did."

"And when he was missing?"

"Nah." He turned toward me. "Maybe you don't know this about him. You should. You all should. But he's what you Zen people call 'in the moment'. He's a hundred percent in what he's doing; then he turns and that's gone. He's the same hundred into the next thing. He does care about some people—He wouldn't have left. But when the opportunity came he was glad to grab it, believe me."

"I don't."

"Why," he said, "you left for years."

I didn't bother wondering how he knew that. It was all I could do to block the stings of the truths, about Mike, about me, to try to see past my illusions, to spot the illusions he was trying to create. I said, "You're lying."

"You think so? There's a shocker."

"You'd never let some kid get a handle on your whole operation. Even Mike. So what's the real truth? You helped him get in college?"

"You want me to tell you I just wanted him gone?"

I glanced at the odometer. "Which senator?"

"Kennedy."

"Odd. Mike went to school in Vermont."

"You're missing the point."

"Point is you're lying."

He shrugged.

"End justifies the means?"

He shrugged again and if I could've made out his expression in the dark I'd've seen disdain. The end here was keeping me from getting any other law to the scene before him. And maybe, I'd be a loss leader to distract Adamé for a few minutes. Whatever Serrano'd told me was no more than the means. *Big surprise.*

The car was rattling forward on the pockmarked pavement. I unlocked my door. Serrano didn't appear to notice.

Ahead, the pavement widened for the final turnoff, the one that veered back. Easy to miss. I could let him go on and—

I drank from the bottle, jostled it putting it back, and unsnapped my seat belt. Again he didn't react, although the noise had been louder. "Slow down," I said to cover it. "Take that left."

He slowed.

My hand was on the door release. In a minute I'd be out and calling the locals.

He was even with the side road.

I eased in the release, bracing my feet to push.

He floored the gas, yanked the wheel so abruptly the wheels flew off the pavement. The car spun to the right, scraped the brush. He pulled the wheel harder, caught it with his knees, freed his hands, and reached between the seats.

I saw his hand come back up, saw the silver metal.

I hit the door release, shoved hard with my feet, and grabbed for the upright doorjamb. I swung out and slammed against the back window of the car. The force knocked the air out. My grip released and I fell.

Just as I heard the shot roar from his gun. *Jesus!*

I skidded across the pavement on one hip, slammed into brush and trees. Dirt filled my eyes, sand strafed my face, nettles ripped at my skin. I scrambled and ran into the woods.

The car slowed, then, suddenly screeched off down the side road toward the Adamé place.

I waited a moment, stunned. Then I made my way back to the road.

The sound of the car grew softer, as he drove away.

I reached into my pocket for my phone.

My pocket was empty.

41

CLOUDS FLOATED OVER the moon. Branches quivered in the wind, leaves scraped, the November night air iced the sweat on my skin. He would have shot me! Now, in the aftermath, it seemed insane that I'd imagined anything else, and yet, even now, it was impossible to connect the Serrano bantering in the car with the Serrano pulling the trigger. Why hadn't he just—

Because he didn't *just*. That's why he was who he was.

He lies all the time. Lies in not merely words.

I could be crumpled by the side of the road bleeding to death.

Like Varine? Like Tessa?

Tessa!

My phone, which had been in my pocket, was nowhere in sight. Finding it would be a colossal stroke of luck, and my luck account was already over-drawn. The house a mile and a half up the road. I started to run. My hip caught, my foot hit the pavement wrong. But I was still enough in shock to ignore pain.

I'd be there in fifteen minutes.

What would Serrano do in that time? He'd ease the car to a stop along the road, open the door silently, slide out, and start to move toward his goal. He still wouldn't know what awaited him.

He wouldn't be stopping to make sure the car was locked.

I ran harder, the ache in my hip throbbing, my ankle silently screaming, and dread closing in. My every step rustled leaves, ruffled grasses, sent unseen little animals scampering, flying. My fear mixed with their fear. Their cries pushed me faster. All I could think about now was Tessa.

He lies all the time.

He couldn't leave me behind at the airport to lead the posse here.

He lies all the time.

I hung on to hope.

The guy'll do anything—anything—for power.

I spotted the car.

I stopped. There was no sound but my own panting and the flutter of leaves in the night wind. I cupped a hand over my mouth, scanned the brush on both sides of the road, then eased the car slowly, carefully open. There was no overhead light. No phone on the seat. None in the glove box. Zip.

Still no sound but the leaves and the scrape of sand. Serrano'd been here fifteen, twenty minutes, time to *do* and get away.

But here sat his car.

The guy'll do anything—anything—for power.

The air was thick with the smell of pine and ocean. Gravel had been dumped onto the two ruts of the driveway. It looked new, not worn in. I made my way, as Serrano must have done, being careful not to step on it. The moon was bright, startlingly so by city standards, but the trees and shrubs were dark. Leaves flickered, shapes behind them shifted. *Only that!* I told myself. No way could anyone be walking through that underbrush and me not hear them.

I stopped, held my breath, tried to name noises. Nothing but rustling. I moved again, careful to place each foot on the grassy cover, not the gravel.

Ahead was a clearing. Beyond it a low building. A house? Dark.

Dark? But empty? That was the question.

I crept to the edge of the clearing. I could never get across it without announcing myself like blinking neon.

The house was twenty yards ahead, an outbuilding to my right, and in front of it a pick-up that could shield me from sight till I figured how to get nearer.

A cloud covered the moon. Taking advantage of the sudden dimness, I slipped behind the truck bed.

The cloud passed, the moonlight lit the yard. It shone on the truck . . . and on the body in the truck bed.

The head was bashed and bloody . . . and bald. I stared for a ridiculously long time before I could make myself understand that the dead man in a pick-up truck in rural North Carolina was Declan Serrano, the cockroach of San Francisco.

Declan Serrano, who'd worked both sides for two decades, who'd survived gang wars and internal affairs investigations, who'd walked my city's streets with impunity, was dead!

Bludgeoned, like the body in my garage back in San Francisco.

Suddenly, I was terrified. The hell with any questions. I needed to get out of here now.

I turned, and gasped.

Her dark hair hung to her chin, her eyes were wide. I could've been back on the bridge.

"Help me!" she screamed.

"HE FOLLOWED ME! I thought I'd be safe here, but he followed me!"
She was shivering in jeans and a short, fitted jacket too thin for the cold.
Her dark hair hung to her chin, her eyes wide. I could've been back on
the bridge. She looked like Tessa Jurovik—stunned, angry, frightened. She
could be Tessa.

I so desperately wanted her to be Tessa, here, alive, not back in San
Francisco—Was this the face I'd looked into for less than a minute, or was
it one I'd never seen in the flesh? Everything froze: her, me, the moment.
What could I see in her that would tell me?

Then the moment passed, and I realized I was coming at this backward.
It didn't matter what I saw in her, because she didn't recognize me at all.
Me, who'd pulled Tessa back from death, who'd been an inch from her face
on the walkway, me, with my long red hair.

Tessa Jurovik was really dead.

Varine Adamé moved and the moon lit her face. She was so much like
Tessa I felt like if I squeezed my eyes shut a couple times, my vision would
clear and there Tessa'd be, not dead in a garage in the Mission district, or
in a morgue drawer.

But it was Varine Adamé standing panicky by the truck.

I expected her to be asking who I was, but she'd moved on from the shock of my arrival and was focused on her own danger. "My husband's going to kill me! He killed this guy! We've got to get away!"

"Why?"

She was looking anxiously at the driveway, the house, the woods, and back to the body in the truck. "You came with him. You—"

"Not by choice."

"What? Never mind. You have a car? You? Him? You've got to have a car."

I was staring at Serrano, too. "He had the keys. What about the truck?"

"Needs gas. Aaron's gone to siphon some. He'll be back in any minute. Find the keys. I'll watch for him. Hurry!"

Wind rustled leaves, shadows fell black and vanished. I wanted to climb into the truck bed, grab the keys, and get the hell out of here. But, Varine? Was Adamé really going to kill her, too? "Why should I believe you?"

"Not now! We've got to get out of here! The keys!"

"Why is Aaron threatening *you?*"

"Ask me questions later, when we're safe. There's no time to—"

"I'm not going anywhere till I get answers. So, why?"

"Because he *thinks* I know all about him. He's sure the cops could squeeze his secrets out of me. He doesn't dare leave me alive. He actually said that to me!"

"And Tessa? What about her?"

"Shh. Look!" She pointed to the driveway.

Automatically I turned and peered into the dark. But her husband wasn't going to be coming up from the road. If he'd been on the road I'd've seen him or at least heard him.

I'd peered a second too long.

"Get up on the damn truck!" The fearful voice was gone. She had a gun.

The charade was over.

But she wasn't going to shoot me, not yet. "Answer me first. Tessa?"

She shifted the gun with ease. If I'd thought of her as a pampered artist, I sure wasn't now.

"Come on! We're not pretending you're going to let me live. So, tell me. Who're you going to brag to if not me?"

She gave a sort of half-snort-half-laugh.

Dammit, I was not going to die without an answer. I prodded. "It was such a good plan, Varine, it must have seemed foolproof. She jumps off the bridge and you're scot-free. Who'd think anyone would come along and save her, cold and foggy as it was there at that time of night?"

She didn't bite. But she didn't stop me either.

"And then your flight got canceled! Otherwise, you would have landed in Miami before she jumped. Varine Adamé'd be 'dead' and you'd have yourself a whole new identity. Isn't that right?"

She so wanted to tell me, to relish, to savor, to—damn her—gloat.

I couldn't stand it. I hit her with, "It was a great plan of Aaron's."

"Fuck Aaron," she screamed. "Aaron's! You think he planned it? Think again! You're like everyone else, you just don't see."

I did see. But I wanted to hear the words from her.

"*I* spotted Tessa. *I* found out what it'd take to buy her. I let her set the price; I didn't haggle. I made sure she wanted it to work."

"But Serrano was convinced Aaron was the mastermind."

Again that half-laugh. "Of course. That's the way it always was. No one gave me a thought, except as an entrée to him. To them I was a cipher. I didn't care—No, I cared and made that work for me. They didn't think— Screw them! Who's the one holding the gun now?"

She aimed that gun at my chest. "Okay, enough. I've gotten my fill of bragging. Now get in that truck and find the keys."

I hoisted myself up onto the bed. Serrano lay on his back, like he'd been at the tailgate about to jump off when the shot had blasted him backward. His chest was a mess. Blood pooled on it around it, splattered onto his face. I could see the keys, but I didn't reach for them. "How'd you even come across Tessa?"

"She was delivering flyers in the Mission."

Where the cockroach put her on display to be grabbed.

"Come on, get the keys! I don't have all night!"

I yanked them out of his pocket and stood up.

"Throw them on the ground."

I threw. Hard.

They hit her nose and eyes.

I leapt, kicked her gut, and slammed her to the ground.

43

ADAMÉ WAS SHARING morgue space with Serrano. I was sorry the cockroach wasn't alive to appreciate the irony. By morning SFPD was on the horn, the feds were on their way, subpoenas for phone and airline records issued. Whether Varine had called Tessa from here or set up a remote arrangement, there'd be a trail. As for Varine herself, she'd clammed up.

I answered questions, gave my statement, and waited to be free to leave. I was as in-the-clear as is possible for someone who'd flown across three time zones to the scene of a double murder. Even so, there was no chance of my getting back to San Francisco for Mike's birthday, much less me with a pie. My luck account was not merely overdrawn, it was closed.

I made my one phone call—a stricture that subsequently was removed—to Mike.

"Darce? We've all been—where the hell are you?"

"Jail." Before he could ask more, I explained about Varine shooting her husband, then Serrano. I skimmed over the details of my arrival on the scene, of danger to me, knowing my brother wouldn't ask now, so he'd be able to report honestly to the family that I'd said nothing about danger. It was a sweet moment of collusion. Later, though, he'd demand every detail. *Later* was when I'd be able to handle that discussion.

He seemed to understand and let the silence linger till I changed the subject. "Listen. There's no way I'm going to make it to your birthday dinner. I—"

"I'm postponing."

"Don't, just for me—"

He laughed. "It's not just for you, trust me. Gracie and Gary've both hinted about food delinquency problems. They'll be ecstatic to postpone. Besides, the tale of you holding up the big event because you're in jail . . . Darce, it's going to be legend."

After we hung up silence wrapped around me, and I sat thinking of Tessa.

In the zendo we do a simple ceremony when a friend dies—we sit zazen, letting thoughts go and returning to the reality of the ever-present moment. Then we chant the Heart Sutra and remember the person we cared about. At some point in that long night I did that for Tessa. When I got back home Kristi and I would go out for a drink and we'd talk of her. There are worse memorials than the shared words of friends.

□ □ □

In the airport in Raleigh-Durham Friday I checked messages for the final time before my flight and dealt with those I'd left unanswered. There were three in that category from Jed Elliot, each less encouraging than its predecessor. His hospital visits to Mac hadn't gone well. How could they have when the topic was the faded illusion of funding? *Faster!* had been on financial life support earlier; now, this last collapse looked fatal. I could have called him back to remind him we'd had funding problems before, but that was a conversation unlikely to make either of us feel any better. Now, at six in the morning—3:00 AM in California—I left a message. Monday I'd contact my agent, update my website, and get to work on a new video for it.

"Someone will meet you at the airport," I was told in one of my many conversations with family members. But when I staggered out to the curb in Oakland I wasn't expecting to see Leo. Leo and Duffy, the Scottie once known as my dog and who, more recently, was being referred to as "the dog Darcy brought Mom."

I plunked my boxes in the back, myself in the passenger seat, and Duffy jumped onto my lap. Already it was a good day.

"I was told you were luggageless. What's in the boxes?"

"Pies, three of them, from the sheriff in North Carolina. One for every time I complained about forgetting to bring a pie. Plus, pork barbecue to die for."

Duffy leapt to the back seat, sniffed seriously, and then, as if having made a difficult executive decision, returned to my lap.

"Leo, I have to say I'm really glad to see you. Much as I love my family, it's great to have this moment of sanity before the dinner tonight. The planning's been so fraught—Awful as the last couple days have been, I was glad to be out of town."

"Expectations." He meant, as opposed to reality.

"Yeah. I kept assuming—*assuming!*"

He laughed.

"Despite everything, I kept on assuming I'd meet Tessa, that things would work out for her. I mean, until—"

He pulled into the slow lane. "One thing you can rely on: Things are as they are."

I nodded. A moment passed and I quoted Suzuki-roshi: "Things change."

"Yes." He meant both were true.

"You know," I said after a bit, "the people I feel worst about are the least real. Despite everything, there were parts of Declan Serrano I liked. I feel like I could have—"

"—created an illusion that would have suited you?"

I nodded again. "And Tessa, with whom I spent less than a minute. Tessa."

Her name hung in the air.

We started up the rise onto the Bay Bridge. Ahead was the San Francisco skyline. And beyond, out of sight, the Golden Gate.

The Golden Gate would always carry Tessa's shadow and how easy it is to step into death.

I looked at Leo. "What is life?"

Duffy shifted and shoved his head impatiently under my hand.

ACKNOWLEDGMENTS

I AM GRATEFUL to stunt coordinator and director Carolyn Day, who is always willing to answer my questions, to writer Linda Grant, my perceptive and gracious first reader and friend, to editor Michele Slung for her hard work and advice. And, as always, special thanks to my superb agent, Dominick Abel.